Finding Shelter

A Rescue Alaska Mystery

by

Kathi Daley

This book is a work of fiction. Names, characters, places, and incidents either are products of the author's imagination or are used fictitiously. Any resemblance to actual events or locales or persons, living or dead, is entirely coincidental.

Copyright © 2021 by Katherine Daley

Version 1.0

All rights reserved, including the right of reproduction in whole or in part in any form.

Chapter 1

I have nightmares. Sometimes they are real.

The storm raged outside the isolated cabin, whistling and humming through small fractures in the old timber walls, which I assumed had once stood sturdy, but over the years had aged and decayed, allowing wisps of air to leak through. Small windows were framed on three of the walls. It appeared as if at one point they might have featured panes of glass, although now they were boarded with thick sheets of plywood, preventing even a small amount of light from seeping through.

I looked around the room and tried to figure out where I was, but nothing seemed familiar.

A splintered table surrounded by four rickety chairs had been placed in the center of the room. If I had to guess, that was the area most used by the inhabitants of the small cabin. There were several tables and a few old lawn chairs set around the room, but there didn't seem to be any electricity. I narrowed my gaze as I tried to take in the entirety of the scene, but the crackling fire and a smattering of oil lanterns that were strategically placed on scarred tables provided the only light in the small dingy room.

I felt a chill run up my spine as I slowly explored the room with my eyes. I knew there must be an opening somewhere, but so far, I couldn't see a way in or a way out.

This was a dream. This had to be a dream. Yet, I felt fully present.

I tried to take a step forward in an attempt to find a door, but my legs felt heavy. Based on the energy exerted for a single step, it felt as if they weighed a hundred pounds apiece. God, I hated dreams where I wanted to move or knew that I needed to run but could barely manage to walk.

Pushing through the anxiety that came with an inability to respond to my natural fight or flight instinct, I slowly looked around the room once again. I knew that I was here for a reason; now, I just needed to have the presence of mind to figure out what that reason might be.

Nothing stood out as being really important. There was an old woman working near what looked to be a small kitchen area. I was sure I'd never met her, and she didn't seem to be in any sort of distress. I watched as she moved from one chore to the next, but nothing stood out as needing my attention or intervention.

I didn't see anyone else in the old wooden cabin, but I supposed someone might be sitting out of my line of sight. Closing my eyes, I tried to enhance my other senses. I could smell the sap burning off the logs in the fire. I could sense the old log walls rattling and shaking with each gust of wind yet the sound they might make as they moved about was unavailable to me for some reason. I could feel the cold seep in through fissures in the wood. I opened my eyes as I realized that if I could get close enough to the cracks in the log walls, I might be able to peek outside and figure out where this cabin stood.

Once again, I tried to move forward, but as had been my previous experience, with each step I tried to take, the heavier my legs became. It was almost as if my legs were not my own.

Perhaps moving toward the wall wasn't that important. My instincts told me it was night, and, therefore, there wouldn't be anything to see even if I should eventually reach my destination. I paused as I tried to decide what to do. The old stone fireplace, which was located on the wall furthest from the door, appeared to hiss and snap as burning logs chased the worst of the chill from the room. Its warmth was welcoming, so I turned slightly and headed in that direction. This time, my legs cooperated.

As I neared the fireplace, I watched the old woman, gnarled and bent with age, dish whatever was heating in the pot on the old woodstove into a bowl with a cracked rim. She set the lid back on the pot before grabbing a spoon from the sink and disappearing down a dark narrow hallway. I hesitated as I focused on the hallway. I wanted to follow but was having a hard time getting started. Eventually, my legs cooperated. As I headed down the shadowy abyss, I had to wonder again about the context of the dream. The hallway I traveled was unlike any I'd ever experienced. This hallway was not only dark, but it seemed endless as well. As I ventured further into the void, the darkness seemed to repel the warmth and light from the outer room.

I stopped walking as I saw the child. I stepped forward and peered around the old woman whose movements I'd been following. I watched as the old woman walked into what appeared to be a bedroom. A young girl, who looked to be around twelve, was sobbing uncontrollably as the old woman approached. I was sure I'd never seen the child before, and I certainly had no idea why she was locked in the room at the end of the void, but while I didn't know her name, I immediately recognized the terror in her eyes.

I could see her mouth moving, but I couldn't hear her words. Her blond hair was stuck to wet cheeks stained with tears. If I had to guess, she was sobbing to be set free.

I waited to see what the old woman would do, but she didn't respond. She didn't make eye contact with the girl or offer comfort or sympathy of any kind. She simply set the bowl she'd brought on the table next to the old iron bed, turned, and walked back into the void.

I didn't follow immediately. I took a minute to watch as the girl shoved the food aside, curled up into a ball, and cried even harder. Sensing the girl's fear, I tried to reach out to her, but when I attempted to speak, I found that I had no voice.

I hated these sorts of dreams. I hated the feeling of helplessness that came from knowing someone was in trouble and wanting to help but being helpless to do so. I tried to reach out to the young girl, willing her to know I was there, but she simply lay on the filthy mattress, with the covers pulled over her head as she tried to hide from her pain.

Once again, I tried to step toward the child, but as I struggled to move forward, I felt myself being pulled back. Back to my small cabin in the woods. Back to the reality in which I lived during my waking hours. Back to the comfort and security that I knew the child in my dream might never again enjoy.

My heart continued to pound as I slowly opened my eyes. The room was dark but familiar. I was lying in my bed. Like in my dream, a storm raged outside, causing the walls of my rustic cabin to rattle as the wind whistled through windows in need of sealing. Sensing my restlessness, my golden retriever, Honey, had worked her way up from the bottom of the bed where she usually slept and laid her head on my chest. I ran my hands through her thick winter coat as my therapy cat, Moose, snuggled in beside me. Unfortunately, vivid dreams were a regular part of my life as of late, and the routine of waking in the middle of one to a pounding heart and cold sweats was an event the animals were becoming used to.

"It's okay," I said aloud as my wolf hybrid, Denali, moved to the bedroom door and began growling deep in his throat. Denali was my protector, and I suspected that although he couldn't sense any real danger, he could sense my distress and duress, which disturbed him. "It was only a dream."

Only a dream.

I rolled the concept around in my mind as my search-and-rescue dog, Yukon, jumped up onto the bed and settled into the spot at the foot of the bed Honey had deserted when she'd crawled up to my side. Had it only been a dream? There'd been a time when the reality I experienced during sleep and the reality I experienced during wakefulness were clearly discernable. But lately, it seemed that the border between my dreams and visions had muddied, leaving me feeling unsettled with every nightmare that invaded my subconscious mind.

Perhaps what I'd just experienced was a sleeping vision. I'd had them before, and each time I had such a vision, my inner voice had been trying to share something important with me. Something I really needed to pay attention to. When I'd first been "gifted" with the ability to sense and actually "see" those I was meant to rescue, my experience had been contained to that specific circumstance. An individual would become lost or injured, and the search-and-rescue team I volunteered for would be called in. I'd focus on the victim, and if I was able to make a connection, more often than not, I was able to help the rest of the team find the person they'd set out to find.

In the beginning, I'd considered my ability to be a gift.

But now? Now that my ability to see the thoughts and movements of others had begun to expand and mutate, I was becoming more and more convinced that my gift was actually a curse.

"Maybe we should just get up," I said to the animals, who were never able to really settle back down after one of my abrupt awakenings.

Yukon jumped down off the bed where he joined my three-legged dog, Lucky, on the floor. I gave Moose a tiny shove so I could work my way toward the edge of the bed, which caused him to jump down onto the floor as well. Denali had already moved into the main room of my small cabin, which caused my husky mix, Shia, to follow him. Grabbing a heavy robe, I slid my feet into knee-high slippers and made my way out of the bedroom and into the main room. Tossing a log on the fire, which had burned down to embers as we slept, I opened the door of the enclosed porch and called my retired sled dogs, Kodi and Juno, inside. I'd tried to train Kodi and Juno to sleep inside the house, but since they'd been brought up as outdoor dogs, they really didn't like spending a lot of time inside next to the heat of the fire. I worried about them as they aged, so I'd moved them from the barn to the porch this winter.

Once the log I'd tossed into the fireplace caught and began to heat the room, I turned my attention to making coffee. As I worked, I thought about the old woman in the cabin and the child, who seemed to be a captive. I wondered once again if the scene I'd experienced had simply been a dream or if it had been something more. If it had been a vision and not a dream, then whose mind had I been connected with?

In the dream or vision, I'd watched the old woman bring food to the girl in the bedroom, but I hadn't been connected with her thoughts or intentions. Likewise, while I'd been able to see the girl in what I was sure was a locked room, I hadn't felt overly connected with her. I'd been able to observe her behavior but not know her thoughts or experience her emotions first hand.

Maybe my gift was growing and evolving once again. That seemed to be the pattern as of late. At first, all I could do was watch the rescue victims who I was meant to help. Then as time passed, I'd developed the ability to actually read their thoughts and feel their pain, although that connection had initially been a one-way connection where I could sense them, yet they couldn't sense my presence in their mind. Eventually, my ability to connect psychically rather than just observing the situation had led to my ability to intentionally and deliberately communicate with others at times.

Of course, the evolution of my gift hadn't stopped progressing there. As time passed, my visions began to leak into my dreams, and many dreams that I experienced became so real that I often awoke crying and shaking.

I supposed as bad as that was, the worst evolution of my gift was the evolution that allowed me to connect, not just with the mind of helpless victims in need of rescuing, but with the minds of vicious killers as well. It was that ability, I was sure, that was causing me to slowly go insane. I suspected it was that ability that had led to the sleepless nights and unending headaches as well.

Once the coffee finished brewing, I settled onto the sofa with a tall mug and wrapped a warm blanket around my shivering body. Honey jumped up onto the sofa and laid her head in my lap. The other dogs settled on rugs in front of the fire. Apparently, this mid-sleep wakefulness had occurred so often over the past few weeks that they recognized the routine. Even Denali, who would usually have remained on high alert had I been startled from sleep before the first rays of light, had happily curled up and gone back to sleep. I had no idea where Moose had wandered off to, but he'd probably gone back to bed. He'd come to me at a time when I'd most needed his ability to center and calm my emotions, but now that the visions and dreams had begun to come so often, I suspected that I was wearing him out.

As I sipped my coffee, I tried to decide if there was something I should do about the dream. If it had just been a dream, then it seemed that now that it had passed, no further action was required, but if the dream had really been a vision...

Of course, even if it had been a vision, I hadn't picked up enough information to help the girl. I knew that she seemed to have been held captive. I knew that she was frightened, but I didn't sense that she'd been injured. I knew that she was being held in a small rustic cabin, although I had no idea where that cabin might be located. In my dream, a storm had been raging outside the cabin, and a storm raged outside the cabin I sat in now, so assuming that the cabin in my dream was an actual place and not a figment of my imagination, perhaps the cabin in my dream was nearby. I tried to hone in on the face of the old woman, but no matter how hard I tried, I couldn't bring her features into focus.

I wanted to help, but I really didn't know how to do that. I supposed I could call my good friend, Police Chief Hank Houston. Houston knew about my ability, and if he had an open missing persons case relating to a young girl with blond hair and huge brown eyes, maybe what I'd seen could help him. Making the decision to call him once he'd arrived at his office, I uncurled myself from the sofa and headed into the kitchen for a second mug of coffee. As I wandered back into the main room, I noticed the light on my answering machine flashing. While most folks in this day and age had replaced their old machine with voicemail connected to their cell phone account, cell service where I lived was spotty at best during a storm, so I had both.

I pushed the button. "You've reached Harmony Carson; please leave a message." I waited for the message to play. "Hey, Harm, it's Harley." Harley Medford was an actor and the benefactor of the Rescue Animal Shelter. Until he came along and donated both the building to house the facility and the cash to run it, Rescue hadn't had a shelter, which is most likely how I'd ended up with so many animals. "I'm not sure if you remember, but I have a movie starting this month, so I'll be out of town for eight to ten weeks. We discussed the fact that you'll need to spend additional time at the shelter during my absence. I hope that's still okay. Call me anytime on my cell phone. If I can't answer, I'll call you back when I can. Love you."

As the message ended, I thought about my absolutely gorgeous, kind, and generous friend. There was a time when I was sure he was the man of my dreams, but since Harley had moved back to Rescue and I'd begun spending a lot of time with him, I realized we really were better off as friends. Close friends. Best friends. But friends all the same.

It was much too early to call Harley back, so I grabbed my cell phone, which actually had bars for once, and texted him to let him know that I'd gotten his message and would handle everything while he was away. Between my job at Neverland, the bar and grill my brother-in-law, Jake Cartwright, owned, and my time at the shelter, which was the enterprise nearest and dearest to my heart, I was going to be a busy woman. I just hoped the dream that had interrupted my sleep early this morning would resolve itself before I went completely insane.

Chapter 2

It had almost been a week since I'd had the first dream about the old woman in the cabin taking food to the girl who seemed to be held captive in a room with a bed but no other comforts. I still didn't know who I'd been channeling, but by this point, I was pretty sure the nightly visions were just that and not random dreams baked up in my subconscious. I'd shared my visions with Houston, hoping that he'd be able to find the girl whose horror I'd been sharing, but so far, he'd been unsuccessful.

As with the first dream, the girl in the dreams that followed hadn't seemed to be injured. She'd been scared, but the terror I'd seen in her eyes that first time seemed to have dissipated a bit. I supposed that she was adapting to her situation. Not that she'd ever really be able to adapt to being locked in a dark room in a cold cabin with no one for company other than an old woman who brought her unappetizing looking soup or stew. But at least she no longer seemed to be fighting her reality the way she had the first few times.

"You look awful," Jake said after I'd shown up for my shift at Neverland.

"Thanks. You look lovely as well," I shot back.

"Still having the dreams?" he asked while wiping down the smooth wooden surface of the bar.

I nodded. "Every night."

"Are they the same each night?" he asked.

I took a deep breath and blew it out slowly. "Mostly. I enter the dream each night just as an old woman prepares to bring food to a girl who seems to be locked in a bedroom, which is down a dark hallway. The hallway is unusually long and unusually dark, so I don't think I'm experiencing an actual hallway. I think it's more of a representation of the barrier between the shabby but warm and even somewhat inviting room where the food is prepared and the cold, barren room where the girl is being kept." I paused to take a breath and then continued. "Each night, I watch as the old woman ladles some sort of soup or stew into a bowl, grabs a spoon from the sink, and then heads down the hallway to deliver the meal. Each night, the girl in the room is curled up on the bed. I'm not connected with her psychically, so I can only imagine what she is feeling, but she looks cold and frightened."

"Has the girl been injured?"

I slowly shook my head. "Not that I can tell. She's scared and sad, but I haven't noticed any blood or bruising. Of course, I have no way at this point to know what happens during the time I'm not there as an observer."

"And you still don't know who it is you're channeling?"

"No," I answered. "I can see the old woman, but I can't feel her experiences or read her thoughts, so I don't think it's her mind I'm visiting. The same is true with the girl. I can see what's happening to her during my visits, but I can't feel her pain or her fear. I can only observe it. I feel like there must be a third person in the cabin, but even if there is, why would this person follow the old woman down the hallway, and why wouldn't the girl acknowledge this person's presence once he or she arrives with the old woman. The whole thing really does feel more like a dream than a vision, and I initially believed that was what was going on, but the dreams are so regular, and the headaches left behind have lingered." I put my hand to my head. "I really don't know what to do at this point."

"And Houston still hasn't found a missing persons report for a girl matching the description of the girl in your dreams?"

I shook my head. "No one who matches the description of the girl in my dreams has been reported missing. At least not from this area or from any of the nearby towns. Houston offered to expand his search, but I guess that at this point, I'm still hanging onto a thread of hope that maybe what I'm experiencing is a dream and not a vision. If it is a vision, it's different than any I've ever experienced. If it's a dream, I'd hate to have Houston spend so much time hunting down someone who only exists in my imagination."

Jake put his hand on my shoulder and gave it a squeeze. "I can probably handle things here if you want to go home."

"Thanks, but I'll stay. I don't want to fall asleep too early. I'm hoping that if I'm tired enough, I'll sleep soundly. I figure that keeping busy is the best course of action at this point."

"Okay." He pulled me in for a hug. "If you change your mind and decide you want to leave early, I'll cover for you. If it gets too busy, I'll call the house and have Jordan come over to help out."

Not only was Jordan Fairchild Jake's girlfriend, but she was also a doctor and a member of the search-and-rescue team.

"Thanks. I'll let you know if I decide I can't stay awake. I'm doing okay now, but I did get up early for my volunteer shift at the shelter."

Jake took a sip of the coffee he always seemed to have at hand. "I'm sure Harley will understand if you decide that you need some time off."

"Harley is making a movie. He won't be back for at least a month. Maybe two. Serena has been handling the desk most of the time, but even she needs breaks, so I've been filling in as much as I can." Serena Walters was our number one volunteer, next to me, of course.

"Did Harley take Brando with him?" Jake asked about the dog Harley had adopted from the shelter two Christmases ago.

"He did. Brando has been doing really well with his training, and I think Harley feels much more comfortable as his handler at this point. Harley has a motorhome for his exclusive use when he's on the set, so he's been taking Brando along when he films and just leaves him there. According to Harley, the cast and crew love the huge puppy, so Brando has been getting a lot of attention even when Harley is busy."

"I'm glad it worked out. I wasn't sure it was the best idea for Harley to adopt a rambunctious puppy when you first foisted the pup on him."

"I didn't foist Brando on Harley," I defended.

Jake lifted a brow.

"Okay, maybe I did, but Harley lives alone. He needed a companion."

"Harley is a very famous action star. I'm sure if he wanted a companion, he could have one," Jake pointed out.

I wrinkled my nose. "Not that kind of companion. Harley needed someone to go home to every night. Someone who would always be there for him. Someone who would love him even if he wasn't rich, gorgeous, and famous."

Jake laughed. "It sounds like that someone might be you."

An image of Houston flashed through my mind. "No. I do love Harley. He's such a great guy, and we have a history of sorts, but I think of him as my best friend." I smiled. "Second to you, of course."

He shrugged. "Of course. You and I are family. There's no one closer than someone you're related to even if you're only related by marriage."

I felt a moment of melancholy as I remembered my sister, Val. If not for her marriage to Jake, he most likely wouldn't be part of my life. I missed Val more than I could say, but after her death, Jake had taken me in and helped me to move on, and I had to admit that most days, I really was happy with the way my life had turned out.

I hugged Jake one more time before moving toward the back room to store the small backpack I used as a purse and grab a clean apron. Waiting tables at Neverland wasn't a glamorous job, but it was a flexible job that allowed me the time I needed to volunteer at the animal shelter and to do whatever the search-and-rescue team required. Jake was good about giving me as much time off as I needed to deal with whatever was going on in my somewhat complicated life.

By the time I returned to the bar and grill's main dining area, Jake was in the kitchen, discussing the daily specials with Sarge. Sarge was former military, a heck of a good cook, and one of Jake's best friends. I waved at both men and then headed toward the bar.

"Hey, Harm," the bartender and search-and-rescue volunteer, Wyatt Forrester, greeted. "You look like death warmed over. Still not sleeping?"

I really wished everyone would stop saying I looked awful. I didn't look that bad. Did I?

"I'm fine. Just tired."

"Still having the dreams?"

I yawned as I nodded.

"Still have no idea why you're having the dreams?"

I shook my head. "I assume I'm supposed to figure out a way to help the girl who's locked in the bedroom, but she isn't the one I'm channeling, so I'm not even sure about that. I can see her, but I can't feel her."

"And you still have no idea where the cabin in your dreams might be located?"

"No." I sighed. "I've tried to look around for clues, but the movements I make in my dreams seem to be controlled by someone else. It's like I'm watching events unfold through this third person's eyes, but I can't read their thoughts or experience their emotions. It's almost like my presence is known to the individual I'm connecting with each night, and they're only allowing me to see and experience what they want me to see and experience and nothing more."

"So you don't have free will?"

I narrowed my gaze. "No. Not really. I experience the event unfolding as if I'm simply a spectator. I can't seem to control things. It occurred to me a couple of nights ago to try to go to the door. I figured that if I could open it, I could look outside. The windows are boarded up, so getting a peek of the cabin's exterior hasn't been possible. I hoped if I could open the door, I'd recognize something, but once I'd had the intention and tried to move, instead of moving toward the door, I found myself following the old woman down the long dark hallway again."

He began checking and replacing the bottles of alcohol that were low. "Do you think the cabin is real or just a manifestation of some sort?"

"I'm not sure," I admitted. "The cabin seems real, but that hallway can't be real. The cabin is small, really just a single room plus whatever is down the hallway, but the hallway is long. Really long. Spatially, the whole thing is off. As I've already mentioned more than once, this dream is unlike any I've had before."

"In what way?"

"As you know, I've had visions that have presented themselves as dreams previously, but in the past, I've experienced events through the eyes of the victim. I can feel what they feel. See what they see. Know what they know. But this is different. As I mentioned, I can see the old woman and the girl, but I'm not connected with them. Yet, I do feel connected with someone. When I wake, I remember fear and longing. It feels like I've experienced the dream on a more intimate level than that of a simple observer, but

I can't figure out whose experience I'm connecting with. The whole thing is very odd."

Wyatt offered me a look of sympathy. "Not knowing with any certainty if there's a real girl out there needing your help or if the whole thing only exists in your head must be making you crazy."

"It *is* making me crazy. Houston has been looking, but he hasn't found anything. It seems that if a young girl was missing, there would be someone looking for her, and Houston would have found a missing persons report. This makes me think the whole thing might really be a dream, but it feels so real." I put a hand to my head. "And the headaches are very much real. In fact, they remind me of the headaches I've had when I've connected with the killer and not the victim."

"Do you think that's what is going on?" Wyatt asked.

I frowned. "I don't know. It seems unlikely that the person who actually did the kidnapping, assuming the kidnapper isn't the old woman who's taking care of the girl, would follow the old woman down the hallway when she delivers the food."

"You did say that the hallway seemed to be more of a representation of something else than an actual hallway."

I bit down on my lower lip softly. "That's true. I suppose the whole thing, the cabin, the old woman, even the girl in the room, might be a representation of something else, but a representation of what?"

Wyatt slowly shook his head. "Man, I wish I knew. I can't imagine what it must be like to have someone visiting your dreams every night and have no idea who they are or what they want. No wonder you have headaches."

"Yeah," I thought to myself. "No wonder." I picked up a rag and began wiping tables. They'd been wiped before closing the evening before and really didn't need wiping again, but I needed to do something to keep myself moving, and wiping tables seemed like a mindless chore. As I looked out on the frozen lake beyond the bar, I considered the idea that perhaps it was the individual who'd kidnapped and imprisoned the girl whose eyes I'd been viewing the scene through. I couldn't imagine why anyone, other than the person who took the girl, would be in the room, but I felt fear and sadness rather than rage and pain when I experienced the dream. In the past, when I'd connected with the killer, the rage and pain I'd experienced had been so intense that there was little doubt in my mind whose thoughts I was sharing.

Sarge walked up behind me as I was wiping the table closest to the huge picture window on the meadow side of the bar. "I brought you some chowder," he said.

I looked at the bowl of thick Alaskan Salmon Chowder and the basket of hot bread he held. "It looks delicious, but I'm really not all that hungry."

"Eat," he said in a tone that left no room for argument.

"Okay, but sit with me while I eat. It's been forever since we had a nice long chat."

Sarge nodded and sat down across from where he'd set the food. "Jake said you're still having the dreams."

I took a bite of the thick, rich chowder, nodding as I did so. "Every night."

"Anything new with each new dream?"

I slowly shook my head. "Not really. Although I do seem to be lingering in the dream longer. I enter the scene earlier in the script. Last night, I watched as the old woman who brings the soup or stew to the girl busied herself in the kitchen for quite a while before attending to her chore." I took a bite of the chowder and then continued. "In the first dream, I hesitated before following her down the long dark hallway, but now that I know what is expected, I follow right away. Each night, the old woman's movements are the same; it's almost as if I'm watching a scene that had been taped and rerun, but the motion of the girl is different, seeming to indicate that I'm watching the scene live."

"Different how?" Sarge asked, picking up a hot roll and buttering it.

"The first night I had the dream, my experience with the girl didn't last long. The girl was obviously terrified. The old woman offered her food, which she turned down, choosing instead to pull the covers over her head and hide." I accepted the buttered roll Sarge handed to me. "As the week has progressed, the actions of the girl have changed. She's more accepting of the food and the old woman. Don't get me wrong. She still seems frightened, but she's no longer crying each time the old woman comes into the room. She almost seems happy to see her and has begun accepting and hungrily eating the food."

"So she's adapting to her circumstances."

I nodded. "Yes. That seems to be the case."

"Does she seem to be afraid of the old woman with the food?" Sarge asked.

"No. Not anymore. She was at first. In fact, she seemed to be terrified when the old woman showed up, but now I sense acceptance of her presence." I lifted my glass of water and took a sip. "As I mentioned, I'm not channeling the girl, so I can't actually feel what she's feeling, but I no longer sense the fear I sensed that first night."

"Do you think she's being abused?" Sarge asked.

I slowly shook my head. "No. I don't think so. I'm only present for this one small part of her day, and I can't hear her thoughts, but she doesn't seem to be in any sort of physical distress. She is locked in the room, and I'm sure that can't be pleasant, but she's free to move around the room. I haven't noticed any cuts or bruising, and I don't sense that she's been sexually assaulted, although I can't know any of this with any certainty. She seems unhappy but no longer terrified. I'd say she is definitely adapting to her circumstances."

Sarge crossed his arms on the table in front of him. "Kids are adaptable, and I suppose as long as the girl in your dreams hasn't had to endure any sort of physical pain, she might be allowing herself to settle into her new circumstances. Self-preservation is a powerful thing. It's a drive that can make all the difference between a life that is tolerable and one that isn't."

I tore off a piece of the roll. "Yeah. That's my sense. I just wish I knew why I'm having the dreams and how I can help her."

"Based on what I know from watching you work all these years, there's a reason you're having the dreams, and while that reason might not be clear at this moment, if you're patient and open to whatever message is trying to make itself known, you'll figure it out."

"You're right. I know you're right, but given the circumstances, it's hard to be patient." I pushed the mostly empty bowl to the center of the table. "That was delicious, but I'm stuffed. The after-work crowd should be arriving soon, so I guess I should head to the back and wash up. Thanks for the food and the conversation."

"Any time, darlin'. You know ol' Sarge is always here for you."

Chapter 3

The dream this morning was different. For one thing, the cabin, while similar, wasn't the same. As with the other cabin, this one was small. A single room with a living area and a small kitchen, but not much more. The windows on both cabins were boarded, but the interior of the rooms and furnishings were different. The old stone fireplace from the first cabin had been replaced with one of brick, and the old woodstove was a little bigger and a bit more modern than the first one. While the first cabin had featured a table and chairs in front of the fireplace, this new cabin had an old sofa and coffee table.

But some things were the same as well. The room was still dark, with the exception of the light from the fireplace and several oil lamps. And it was still cold if you ventured too far away from the fireplace. The old woman looked the same, and as she had before, she'd been busying herself in the small kitchen area when I'd first arrived. As she had in the past, once her chores in the kitchen were completed, she headed to the old woodstove where she had something heating in a pot.

I thought back over the dreams I'd had in the past week and tried to compare every detail. So far, while this cabin was different, the old woman was the same. If the script she'd been following was adhered to again, I knew that once she'd ladled the soup or stew into the cracked bowl, she'd head over to the sink, grab a spoon, and then head down a long dark corridor until she reached a heavy wooden door. She'd take a key from the pocket of her apron, open the door, and bring the bowl into the room. She'd hand the bowl to the girl and then leave.

As I watched the old woman ladle the soup or stew into the bowl during this dream, however, I noticed something alarming. While she had initially followed the script, this time when she ladled the soup or stew, she filled two bowls.

"A second victim?" I asked myself as I followed the old woman down a long dark hallway, which was very similar to the first one. I watched as she took out her key, unlocked the door, and then pushed it wide enough to reveal two girls in the little room with a single bed.

The girl with the blond hair, who I'd been visiting all week, was hugging and attempting to comfort a girl that looked to be close to her own age but had brown hair. When the old woman offered the food to the girls, the new girl cowered in the corner, but the blond-haired girl accepted both bowls.

The dogs had become so used to my nightly terrors that they barely even stirred when I got up. I picked my cell phone up off the bedside table, sighed in relief when I realized I had bars, and called Houston despite the fact it was only three a.m.

"Harmony?" Houston asked in a groggy tone of voice after the phone had rung at least six times.

"There was a second girl this morning. The new girl had dark hair. We couldn't find the blond-haired girl in the missing persons file, but maybe we can find the dark-haired girl."

"A second girl?"

"That's what I just said. I know it's early, but this might be the lead we've been waiting for. You need to wake up."

"I'm awake," he assured me. "Anything else?"

"The cabin was different in this dream. Similar, but different. If my visions are based in some sort of reality, then I'm going to say that whoever is taking these girls moved the first one before taking the second."

"But you don't know where the new cabin is located?"

"No. The windows are boarded up." I paused to think about it. "There are a ton of seasonal cabins littered across the entire state. They're rented out to hunters and outdoorsmen in the summer but boarded up in the winter. What if whoever is taking the girls is making use of those cabins?"

"That does make sense."

"In my dream, there's always a fireplace, but there doesn't seem to be any electricity. That would fit the seasonal cabin theory as well since I know water and electricity for the seasonal cabins are usually turned off in the winter."

"The old woman makes soup or stew. She must have water," Houston pointed out.

"She probably melts some snow."

I waited for Houston to reply. I was sure I'd heard him yawn. Eventually, he spoke. "Put on some coffee. Kojak and I will be there in thirty minutes." Houston referred to his dog.

I got up, pulled on some warm clothes, and let the dogs out for a bathroom break while I got a fire started and made coffee. Usually, I headed over to the barn to feed my blind mule, Homer, and the rest of the animals after having my first mug of coffee, but it was early, and I figured that could wait until after Houston and I chatted. I really hoped that Houston would be able to come up with some information on the dark-haired girl. Knowing who she was and where she'd been taken from would help us narrow down where the cabins in my dreams might actually exist. Assuming, of course, that they did actually exist, and I wasn't losing my mind, which given the massive headaches I'd been having, combined with my lack of sleep, seemed equally as likely as the alternative.

When Houston arrived, he not only had his rescue dog, Kojak, in tow but his laptop as well. After accepting a mug of dark rich coffee, he logged on and pulled up a file that seemed to contain missing persons reports from across the state. We knew the dark-haired girl had just arrived in this morning's dream, which seemed to indicate that she'd most likely been kidnapped within the past twenty-four to forty-eight hours.

"That's her," I said, pointing to the screen. "That's the second girl in my dream."

"Bella Smothers," Houston read. "She's twelve years old and went missing while walking home after an after-school piano lesson two days ago."

"Two days?" I asked. "I wonder why she just now showed up in the dream." I focused on the image on the screen. "Does she live in Rescue?"

"Tok."

"Tok? I guess I just assumed the missing girls were from this immediate area."

"The cabins the kidnapper is using might be in this area, but apparently, the newest girl is from a town east of here." Houston frowned. "I wonder if that's why I didn't find a missing persons report for the first girl. Maybe she was taken from a town even further away."

"I thought you did a search for the entire state."

"I did. But I didn't look for missing twelve-year-olds in Canada. Tok is less than a hundred miles from the Canadian border. What if the first girl was picked up across the border? What if the first cabin was across the border? Maybe our kidnapper is moving west."

I frowned. "Moving west? You think this guy kidnaped the blond-haired girl, held her for a week or so near the town where she was abducted, and then moved her to a new location where he kidnapped the second girl?"

"I think it's more likely that he kidnapped the first girl, moved her to a distant location, kidnapped the second girl, and then moved them both to a new location."

"Yeah. I guess it makes sense that the man would move after the kidnapping took place. The first girl might have been taken from somewhere in Canada, but the first cabin might have been near Tok. Once he took the second girl, he must have taken both girls and the old woman to wherever the second cabin in my dream is located." I looked at Houston. "Do you think he's done? Do you think he'll take a third girl and then a fourth?"

"I don't know," he admitted.

"I guess it makes sense to expand your search." I looked at the screen again. The girl in the photo was happy and smiling, but the girl in my dream had been terrified. "We need to find her, and we need to find her fast."

"I agree. I'll look for a blond-haired girl who's missing in Canada, and I'll set up a search grid now that we have confirmation that your dreams are real. We know the second girl was taken in Tok, which gives us a starting point. If we can find the location of the first abduction, it will give us additional data as to how far he travels between kidnappings."

"Do you think the blond-haired girl was his first?" I hated to consider what might have happened to the others had there been others, but it seemed negligent on our part not to assume that the blond-haired girl might not have been the first.

"I don't know. I hope the two girls we know about are the only girls who have been taken, but I think it's likely there could have been other girls. I'm going to widen my search parameters for girls in the ten to fourteen year age range who've gone missing over the last five years from either the US or Canada who have never been found. It's going to bring up a lot of cases, but if there were other girls who fit the pattern, then it will be good to know that."

"What about the old woman? I know we don't have much, but maybe someone is looking for her. Maybe there's a missing persons report or something."

"You said she was old. How old?"

I shrugged. "I guess she's in her seventies or eighties. She has totally white hair that's pulled back into a bun at the base of her neck. She's petite and almost frail. I don't remember noticing her eye color. I really only have a small glimpse of her each night, and she never says anything."

"What does she do exactly?"

"After moving around the kitchen a bit, she ladles whatever it is that she's cooking on an old woodstove into a bowl and brings it to the room where the blond-haired girl is being kept. In the latest dream, the old woman filled two bowls and took them to a different room where both girls are being kept. Once she delivers the food, she leaves."

"What is she wearing?"

I closed my eyes and tried to pull the image to the surface. "A dress. An everyday housedress like my great-grandmother used to wear. It's long with long sleeves."

"Color?"

"Gray. A sort of medium gray. No pattern. Pretty drab, but serviceable."

"Has she worn the same thing each time you've had a dream?"

My eyes flew open. "Yes. Every single time. That's odd, right? If the visions are taking place across time, then she should be changing her clothes."

"That would seem to be the case," he agreed. "Unless the old woman isn't actually real. Maybe she's a manifestation of whoever you're channeling. Maybe this person, who seems to be in control of what you see, is feeding you prerecorded scripts."

I frowned. "Prerecorded?"

"You've had all the dreams late at night or early in the morning. Today, you called me around three a.m. If the visions were live, then either the dreams are memories stored in the mind of whoever you're channeling, this old woman is feeding these girls in the middle of the night, or the cabins you see in your dreams are in Greenland or somewhere in a much different time zone."

"You make a good point. I hadn't thought of that. The second girl was taken in Tok. I think we should assume that at least one of the two cabins is located in close proximity to Tok. I'm not sure why the glitch in the timeline hadn't occurred to me." I paused to think about it. "I suppose the dreams may even be memories from a day before the one I'm experiencing. But if that's true, why is whoever I'm connected with feeding me reruns?"

"I don't know. This whole thing is really confusing to me. What I do know is that you 'saw' an actual twelve-year-old who went missing two days ago. To me, that is real and understandable. My number one priority at this point is to find the girl and the cabin in which she is being held, which I intend to do." He reached out and tucked a lock of my hair behind my ear. "I think that you should try to get some sleep."

"I'm fine."

"No offense, but you don't look fine. In fact, you look very un-fine to me."

"Is that your clever way of telling me I look awful?"

He smiled but didn't respond.

"Jake, Wyatt, Sarge, and five of my regulars at the bar said the same thing to me during my shift, only they were a bit blunter about it." I ran a hand over my face. "Maybe I will liy down for a bit. I'll be heading to the animal shelter later, so if you find something, give me a call on my cell phone. I'll probably be away from the cabin for most of the day."

Houston put his hands on my shoulders. He pulled me forward and kissed me on top of my head. "Don't worry," he said, pulling me in for a hug. "We'll find these girls, and when we do, the headaches and the sleepless nights should come to an end."

"I hope so," I said as I put my arms around his waist and soaked in the comfort of his embrace.

Chapter 4

When I arrived at the shelter, I found Serena kneeling in front of a box that appeared to have been left on the walkway bordering the front door. "What do you have there?" I asked.

"Kittens."

"Kittens?"

She nodded. "Six of them, three black, one orange, one white, and one gray. I'm afraid I tore the top when I opened the box, rendering it useless as a barrier. I was just about to bring the little tykes inside, but the box got wet, and I'm afraid it will fall apart if I lift it. I was trying to figure out a way to take a few kittens at a time without the others getting out and getting away, but now that you're here, you can help me."

"I'll open the front door and block it open. Once I do that, I'll grab three, and you can grab three. How old are they?"

"They look to be four or five weeks old. Probably closer to five. They sure are cute."

I peeked into the box. "Yes, they are. And they have nice long fur, but it's freezing out here, so let's get them inside before we all freeze."

Once we got all six kittens inside and into a large cage, we called the local veterinarian to come by and look at them, as was our standard procedure for all new arrivals. Once she'd been by and given us her opinion of the situation, we would be able to make a plan for the kittens' treatment, care, and eventual rehoming. I really couldn't imagine what sort of person would tape six kittens into a box and then leave them out in the cold, but they looked to have been fed and well cared for before arriving, so perhaps whoever had been taking care of them had found themselves in an impossible situation and had done what they could. Still, I would have preferred that they'd dropped the kittens off during business hours when someone was here to take them in, but I supposed they might have been left in a less friendly environment, so I'd just be grateful we had them now and not worry about the rest.

"Did the man who called about dropping off the husky ever come by yesterday?" I asked Serena as we settled the kittens in their temporary home.

"Actually, he called back and said that his buddy decided to take him, so he wouldn't be surrendering him after all."

"That's good. Hopefully, the dog will have a good home with his friend. It really is too bad the guy who originally owned him had to move and couldn't take him along. I'm sure the separation will be hard on both the man and the dog."

"Yeah. I got the feeling the man was unhappy about the situation, but he did say that his buddy will take good care of him." She nodded her head toward a stack of boxes piled against a nearby wall. "Those heated dog beds that Harley ordered before he left came in."

I glanced at the boxes. "That's wonderful. The beds we have are getting worn."

"The way Harley really cares about the animals is so nice. I mean, the guy is rich and famous and lives a really big life, yet he took the time to personally order and pay for dog beds before he left."

"Harley is a nice guy," I agreed.

"I can't believe he's still single. It seems like he could have his choice of women, and yet he seems pretty committed to the bachelor lifestyle."

I paused and looked at Serena. "Harley seems really happy with the life he's mapped out, but he lives a duel life that wouldn't appeal to a lot of women. When he's not working, he lives here in Rescue. That's a hard sale with most women, even for a great guy like Harley. And if he did find someone who was into the Alaskan lifestyle, odds are that same woman would hate life in Hollywood, where he spends the other half of his life. And then there is all the traveling…"

"Yeah. I get what you're saying. Most Hollywood women aren't Alaska women and vice versa. Still, I hate to see Harley alone."

"He's not alone. Harley has Brando, who he adores, and when he's here in Rescue, he has all of us."

"Yeah, I guess." Serena finished settling the kittens and then began opening the boxes with the new dog beds. "Do you want to save the old beds as they're replaced or recycle them?"

"Let's keep a few as backups and recycle the others. I know several of the old beds are little more than rags at this point."

"The dogs do tend to be hard on them. Most of the beds are less than a year old. I guess the dogs get bored during the winter and look for anything they can find to chew on. I'll make sure everyone has an approved chew toy." Serena opened the box next in the stack. "Oh, look. A box of chew toys. Harley really did think of everything."

I recognized that look in Serena's eyes. I'd had that look for a lot of years. She was falling for the man we both cared a lot about. I hoped the talk we'd just had about Harley's multiple lifestyles had really sunk in. Serena would hate the Hollywood lifestyle, and despite the fact that Harley spent a lot of time in Rescue, it was my impression that he was far from ready to leave his movie star life behind and settle down.

Once the boxes had been unpacked, Serena headed to the back to clean cages, and I set to work feeding everyone and making sure they had fresh water. We'd had several very successful adoption events during the fall and holiday season, so the number of residents we were currently caring for had been reduced by half of what it had been during the summer. Opening an animal shelter in Rescue had been a dream of mine long before Harley wandered back into my life and made all my dreams come true. I really did owe him a lot, and under a different set of circumstances, the two of us might even have developed a romantic relationship, but as I'd just tried to remind Serena, Harley had one foot planted in Alaska and one foot planted in Hollywood, while I most definitely had both feet firmly planted right here in Rescue. If, and when, I entered into a relationship of the romantic kind, it would be with a man who was as firmly rooted in Rescue as I was.

Not that I was looking for a man. I most definitely wasn't. Like Harley, I'd carved out a life that I loved. I had my cabin and my animals. I had the animal shelter. I had Jake and the bar. I had the search-and-rescue team and the long hours that came with my participation on the team. Even more importantly, I had friends. Good friends. Friends who meant a lot to me. Friends who filled most, if not all, the little nooks and crannies of my life. Most days, I felt that I had a life most could only dream of. Still, if I was perfectly honest, I supposed there were times late at night when a longing to snuggle up with someone who wasn't covered in fur would come over me, and I'd wonder what a life shared with a special someone might be like.

Chapter 5

By the following day, Houston still hadn't figured out who the old woman was, but he'd expanded his search for the blond-haired girl I'd first seen in my dreams and was following up with some leads. None of the missing girls that he'd identified as possible matches lived in Alaska, but given what we suspected about the kidnapper's movements, he'd decided to look at Canada and the West Coast of the US as well.

I'd had the dream again last night, although I was so exhausted from my lack of sleep that I had actually managed to get a couple more hours of shut-eye once the dream had passed. Houston had suggested that I write everything down that I remembered from the dream upon waking, so I'd placed a pen and notepad next to the bed and desperately tried to remember if my dream had revealed any information that I hadn't already had.

The routine followed by the old woman had been the same as it had been every night. As she had the previous evening, she'd prepared two bowls of food and brought them into the room where both girls were being held. The blond-haired girl appeared to thank her for the food and then encouraged the other girl, who looked terrified, but was no longer crying, to take the food since it was likely to be the only food they would receive until the following day.

There wasn't a lot of new information revealed in my latest dream, but I did notice something that I hadn't seen before. After the old woman dished up the bowls of soup or stew, she looked toward the front door. It was just a quick glance. She didn't seem to wait or linger. She just glanced up and then continued with her task. Still, even the quick glance was enough to stoke my curiosity.

It was almost as if she'd heard something. I tried to remember if I'd heard any sounds coming from beyond the barrier to the outside. If a sound had caught the old woman's attention, it could have been a person preparing to enter the cabin, the wind, or even an animal who'd wandered close enough to be heard. I supposed that unless I could remember a sound, I'd never know what it had been.

It wasn't until I was walking the dogs later that day that I found my answer in the form of a rumbling that echoed through the valley from the summit, which was actually more than fifteen miles away on the other side of the long valley that was bordered by mountains.

"Avalanche control," I said aloud to the dogs, as Denali growled and Yukon barked. We'd had a heavy wet snow a few days ago, followed by a warming trend, only to be topped off by another much heavier snowstorm. Everyone who lived in the area knew that the deep snowpack combined with the warmer conditions and even heavier snow on top was a recipe for an avalanche. When this situation occurred in areas where there were roads or ski hills, small explosions were intentionally set off to cause controlled avalanches, which theoretically would relieve the buildup and prevent a naturally occurring avalanche that might cost the loss of human lives from happening.

I reached down to pat Honey's head in an offer of comfort when the image of the old woman from my dream glancing at the door flashed into my mind.

"She heard the cannon," I said, realizing that this could be a real clue. I hadn't heard the cannon in the dream, but I had felt the vibration in the floor. I was sure the reason she'd looked up was due to a sound inaudible to me but real to her.

Of course, the canon she'd heard wouldn't have been the one I'd just heard since I'd had the dream and witnessed her being startled by the rumbling explosion last night. Avalanche control had been going on for the past few days, so perhaps if Houston could track down where explosions had been set off during the past couple of days, it might give us a place to start the search for the cabin the kidnapper was currently using.

Of course, even as I reached for my cell phone, it occurred to me how far sound traveled. The search areas created by taking into account the ability to hear the blasts or feel the vibrations caused by the explosions would be extensive. Still, a clue was a clue, so I made my call.

"Harmony. How are you feeling this afternoon?"

"Good," I lied, feeling overwhelmed, exhausted, and headachy. "The reason I called is because I might have a clue as to the location of the cabin where the girls are currently being held."

"Wonderful. Did you remember something from your dream?"

"Sort of. I remembered that the old woman who brings the food to the girls looked up for a split second before she headed down the hallway in the dream I had last night. As far as I can remember, she's never done that before. She looked toward the front door for a split second and then continued with her routine. Initially, I thought someone was at the door, but she probably would have waited to see who it was, or she might have gone to the door to look for herself if she believed she'd heard a person. Then it occurred to me that she might have heard an animal or perhaps something had been blown into the cabin by the wind creating a thunk. But while I was walking the dogs today, I heard the cannon on the summit. I figure they must be doing avalanche control. When I heard the explosion, I remembered that the old woman in my dream had looked up at the exact time that I'd felt the vibration through the floor. She must have heard the explosion."

"But you didn't hear it in your dream?"

"No. I didn't hear it, but I did feel it."

"So, the cabin must be close to an area where avalanche control procedures have been put into place over the past few days."

"That would be my guess," I said. "Of course, the sound in this area really travels, so even if we can identify the locations of all the explosions over the past couple of days, we'll have a huge area to search."

"Yeah. I agree that finding the cabin will be a longshot, but we finally have a place to start. I'll make some calls and find out where avalanche control measures have been carried out during the past three days. Once we have that, we can look at a map and see if that information tells us anything."

"Okay. The dogs and I are going to head back to the cabin. I'll make dinner if you want to come by."

"Actually, that sounds nice. I'll be there in an hour or two."

After I hung up with Houston, I called the dogs, and we headed back to my cabin. There was a lot of wildlife where I lived, so I liked to keep the dogs close by when we were out and about. Most of the time, the dogs complied with my wishes, but every now and again, Shia, and sometimes Denali, would follow their instincts to chase after whatever animal or threatening sound they may have picked up on.

During the winter, the bears were hibernating, so they didn't pose a threat to man or dog, but there were still wolves and cougars to deal with, which is why, whenever we walked, I had my rifle loaded and ready to expel a warning shot if needed.

Once we arrived back at the cabin, I decided to head to the barn to take care of the animals who lived there. My blind mule, Homer, was the oldest resident of the barn crew. In addition to Homer, there was a cage full of bunnies I'd rescued, a raccoon who'd gone blind, and a baby moose with a broken leg and no sign of a mama who I'd found on one of my walks. The moose was on the mend and would be set free in the spring, but the other animals I currently housed were destined to be with me for the rest of their lives.

I loved the fact that I had the time, space, and resources to take care of so many animals. It was a bit of a challenge if I needed to be away from home overnight, but so far, between Serena from the shelter, Justine from the veterinary hospital, and my best friend, Chloe, I'd always been able to find someone to hold down the fort when I needed to be away.

Once everyone was fed and given fresh water, I headed over to the house to find something to make for dinner. It was winter in Alaska, so the sun had already set despite the fact that my watch told me it was not yet three o'clock. I figured Houston would come around after he did his usual rounds, so I had time to figure out what I would make. I stood in front of my open refrigerator and frowned. Maybe I'd overestimated my supplies when I'd invited him to dinner. Luckily, Houston wasn't a picky eater, and I knew he'd be just as happy with canned soup and a grilled cheese sandwich as he'd be with something that took me hours to prep and even longer to cook.

Settling on chili and cornbread, I began browning the meat, figuring I'd just use canned beans and tomatoes to hurry things along. I had plenty of spices for the chili and all the ingredients for the cornbread, so if I could scrounge up some veggies for a small salad and something to make for dessert, my effort wouldn't be seen as totally unimaginative.

The chili was simmering on the stove by the time Houston arrived. The cornbread was mixed and ready to put in the oven, and I'd washed and diced the veggies for the salad. I'd decided on brownies from a box for dessert. They were baking in the oven when Houston knocked on the front door, so we decided to look at the maps he'd brought while the brownies finished baking. Once they were done, I could swap out the brownies for the cornbread.

"First off, I found our blond-haired girl," he said.

My eyes widened. "You did. Who is she?"

"Her name is Lily Turner. She's eleven years old and was taken from Whitehorse nine days ago."

"So the kidnapper did come through Canada." I looked at the map. "It looks like he might be making his way northwest along route two."

"That's my guess. I spoke to law enforcement in Whitehorse, and they told me that, like Bella, Lily had been walking home alone after participating in an after-school activity. They'd been looking for Lily in the general area of her abduction but hadn't considered that she might have left the country. They still aren't certain how the kidnapper got her past the border patrol, but based on what we think we know, that seems to be the case."

"Okay, so the kidnapper abducted Lily nine days ago in Whitehorse, and then he abducted Bella five days after that in Tok. It's been four days since Bella was abducted. Do you think it's possible that he plans to move on as early as tomorrow?"

"If the five-day span is a pattern and not a random fact, then yes, it does seem likely that he will move to a new location and abduct a new girl as early as tomorrow. That's why time is of the essence in finding the girls."

"Do you have a plan?" I asked.

He nodded, laying a map on the table. "The red dots represent everywhere that avalanche control was executed yesterday and the two days before that. Since you dreamed about the old woman possibly hearing a noise in the background last night, my money is on areas that underwent avalanche control yesterday, but since you said that the dreams seem to be memories you are experiencing rather than live events due to the time of night you experience the dreams, I went back a bit further."

"Only five places," I said. "That seems like it might be a reasonable number of areas to search."

Houston laid a clear map over on top of the one he'd first laid out. "This is a map of seasonal cabins in the area. As you can see, three of the areas that underwent avalanche control also have clumps of cabins within the sound range as determined by pure guesswork."

"Guesswork?"

He shrugged. "Short of an extensive experiment that would require us to set off explosions and then measure the distance in which the sound could be heard, guesswork is all I really have."

I looked down at the map and pointed at one of the areas. "This area underwent avalanche control yesterday, and there are two clusters of cabins in the sound zone. I say we start here."

"I agree. The roads leading out to the cabins are seasonal and currently inaccessible. If the kidnapper did decide to use one of these cabins, he or she must have snowmobiled in. I imagine the fact that the cabins are so isolated will make it easier to determine which, if any, are occupied. But given the tight timeline, I felt it was much too time-consuming to visit each of these areas via snowmobile, so I called Dani, and she agreed to take me up in the bird tomorrow. If any of the cabins in the search grid show signs of life, such as smoke from a fire, then it's likely we've found our kidnapper."

Houston referred to Dani Mathews, a helicopter pilot, valued friend, and member of Rescue's search-and-rescue team.

"I want to go with you," I said.

He nodded. "I figured you would, and Dani's chopper has plenty of room. We only have about six hours of daylight tomorrow, so I plan to meet Dani at first light. If you want to go along, meet us at the helipad at nine-thirty."

"Okay. I'll be there." I glanced at the map again. "The search areas you've identified are really isolated during the winter. Do you really think the kidnapper transported these two girls and the old woman all that way on a snowmobile?"

"If he wanted a safe place to wait out some sort of timeline, then I think he might have. I guess we won't know until we take a look, but at this point, these search areas seem to be our best bet."

Chapter 6

Getting up and ready to leave by nine a.m. was not a problem since I hadn't slept much past three a.m. in weeks. The dream last night had been the same as the others. Based on the cabin I'd experienced in the dream, it seemed as if the group was still in the second cabin, at least for now. It did seem that if the kidnapper followed a specific schedule, the group would most likely move either today or tomorrow. We were so close. I could feel it in my gut. As long as the group stayed put one more day, I really felt like we'd find them. At least I prayed we would. Not only had this whole thing been hard on me, but I couldn't imagine what the kidnapped girls and their families were going through.

After I got up, I made a pot of coffee, showered, and dressed in my warmest clothing. I really had no idea at this point, what the day might bring, but I did suspect that if we found the cabin where the girls were being held, and it was located in an area where Dani couldn't land, there might be snowshoeing involved. Not that snowshoeing was a problem for me. During the winter, I ended up on snowshoes for at least part of almost every day.

Once the dogs had been walked, the cat boxes cleaned, and all the animals fed and given fresh water, I set off for the airfield. I'd flown with Dani many times and knew she was one of the best pilots and that she knew the area like the back of her hand. If the kidnapper was hiding out in the deep forest, she'd find him. Dani was the sort who always got her man, or woman as the case might be.

By the time I arrived at the airfield, Houston had already arrived, and Dani was in the process of warming up the bird. It was early and still dark, but we were working against the clock, and the earlier we got underway, the better. Houston sat in the passenger seat next to Dani while I climbed into the back. We all had a pair of the high-powered binoculars we used for search-and-rescue, and Houston had already gone over the search grid coordinates with Dani. I had a good feeling about finding this guy if he was out there. Or she, I supposed. I'd been imagining the kidnapper as a man, but I supposed at this point, without additional information, we had to assume that either could be true.

By the time we arrived at the first search area, the sun was just cresting the horizon.

"It's lucky that we have clear skies," Dani said.

"That is lucky," I agreed. "Clear skies certainly aren't the norm at this time of the year. If one of the cabins below has a fire going, we should easily be able to see the smoke."

"There are two main clusters of cabins in this area," Houston said. "The cluster to the right is hidden by the umbrella of trees, but we should still be able to see smoke if there is any, and the cluster to the left is just beyond that ridge."

Dani carefully flew back and forth in a search pattern we used for search-and-rescue before we all decided that none of the cabins in this area showed evidence of inhabitation, and it was time to head to the next search grid. I could tell Houston was disappointed that we hadn't found the people we were searching for in the first grouping of cabins. They were closer to the road, and it seemed a lot more likely that if the group had holed up in a seasonal cabin, they'd be found in the group with easy access. The next group of cabins we planned to search was found on the backside of a ski resort. The avalanche control that had been executed at the resort had taken place after the resort had closed for the day, and the guests and employees had left. In my mind, that would put the cannon blast at some point after five o'clock on the evening before I'd had the dream. If the dreams were memories, it still made sense to me that they'd be based on recent memories, so a memory from late in the afternoon or early in the evening before the execution of the dream seemed just about right to me.

When we arrived above the next cluster of cabins, it was evident that the search would be difficult. There were even more trees in the area than there had been with the previous cluster. The only access to the cabins was a road that had been closed after the first snow. The closest access, if one was going to snowmobile in, would be the ski resort. Of course, if the kidnapper had parked in the ski area's parking area, what had he done with his vehicle? It seemed likely that any vehicle left overnight would be tagged and most likely towed by the ski resort's security.

It seemed odd that I'd never seen anyone other than the old woman and the young girls even though I'd visited the two cabins many times. I had to wonder if perhaps the kidnapper had dropped them off and then left them until it was time to move again, which I guessed would explain why a vehicle hadn't been left behind if a snowmobile had been used to access a cabin. The kidnapper would most likely have ferried the old woman and the girls to the cabin one or two at a time and then left them there. I supposed he would have then left the area in the truck or other vehicle that he'd used to tow the snowmobile to the area with a plan to come back for them at some point in the future.

"The tree cover is really thick," Houston said. "My map tells me there are cabins down there, but I don't see them."

"It seems hazier in the northeast section of the search grid," I said. "It could be a random fog patch, but it could also be smoke. Maybe we should take the bird down for a closer look."

Dani did as I suggested and dropped in altitude. As we flew directly over the hazy area, it became apparent that the haze had been caused by smoke.

"We got 'em." Houston said.

"Maybe," I agreed. "It's possible that someone else, a poacher perhaps, has decided to make use of one of the cabins. We'll need to land."

"There's nowhere close for us to do that," Dani said. "The trees in this area are thick, and when you get beyond the tree line, you have the ledge and gorge to deal with." She lifted the bird back toward the altitude she'd been flying at before dipping down for a closer look. "I think our best bet is to land in the parking area at the resort and snowmobile in."

"Jake has a trailer all loaded and ready to go for rescues," I said. "There are four machines on the trailer. He can probably be there in an hour or so."

"I'll radio him," Dani offered. "It's actually still early, so we should have plenty of daylight to get in and out if Jake can come right away."

"We may be riding into a dicey situation. I should call my men for backup," Houston said.

"Unless they have snowmobiles loaded and ready to go, there's no time," I said. "Jake has a gun, and I can handle one as well as any man can. I'll have him bring a backup." I looked at Houston. "You have your gun, so that makes three."

Dani nodded toward a glove box. "I have mine. Four guns and four snowmobiles. Let's go and get those girls."

Luckily, Jake was home and willing to help. He grabbed the guns and snowmobiles and headed in our direction while Dani scouted for the best place to land. She eventually decided on a spot in the overflow parking area. It was close to the forest access we'd need to utilize to begin our journey, and since the lot was used for overflow and not daily operations, it wasn't crowded with vehicles.

After we arrived, Dani began shutting things down. Jake made good time, and he'd arrived within an hour of our contacting him. We all agreed to stay together. After years of participating in search-and-rescues, Jake knew the area better than anyone did, so we headed out with him leading the pack. I fell in behind Jake, Dani fell in behind me, with Houston taking up the rear.

By the time we entered the heavily forested area, we'd found fresh snowmobile tracks. That seemed to confirm that someone was staying in one of the cabins. The fact that the tracks were fresh had caused my heart to constrict a bit. Were we too late? Had they already left? According to the theory Houston and I had worked out, the group would most likely move either today or tomorrow.

Of course, it was still possible that the cabin was being used by poachers, as we'd already speculated. I found my impatience to get to the truth growing with each mile we traveled. As the first of the cabins in the grouping came into view, I knew that one way or another, we'd have our answers in the next few minutes.

Jake stopped his snowmobile when the first cabin in the cluster was reached. Houston pulled up next to him. There was a clear set of snowmobile tracks to follow, so the men decided it was best to leave the snowmobiles and continue on foot. Given the fact that we didn't know what we'd find, it seemed best to approach as quietly as possible, although, in my mind, anyone other than a totally deaf person would have heard us coming for miles.

"There it is," Houston said, pausing as we stood just beyond the tree line from a cabin with smoke still billowing from the chimney.

"I don't see a snowmobile," I said.

"It might be around back," Dani pointed out.

"I'll take the front door," Houston directed. "The three of you come in from the back. I'm not certain that there's a back door, but if I meet with resistance from the front, it will be imperative that the rest of you find a way in."

"The windows are boarded up, but we should be able to pry one of the boards loose if there isn't a back door to access."

Houston nodded, we all took our guns out, removed the safeties, and Jake, Dani, and I headed around to the back while Houston headed toward the front. After a few minutes, I heard Houston call out that it was clear and safe to enter through the front door.

"They aren't here, are they?" I asked, disappointment evident in my voice after Jake, Dani, and I had joined Houston.

He shook his head. "The fire is still hot, so they haven't been gone long."

I looked around the room that featured a tiny kitchen, a small seating area, and a narrow bed. There was a bathroom off the back of the building, but it was basically a studio unit.

"This can't be it," I said. "In my dreams, the girls were in a room that was accessed after traveling down a long hallway. This cabin has no hallway and no bedroom."

"I suppose the kidnapper might have kept the girls in one of the other cabins," Dani said. "Maybe the hallway you traveled wasn't really a hallway. Maybe it was a path between cabins. You told me from the beginning that the hallway didn't seem to be an actual hallway."

"That's true." I opened the front door and stepped outside. I looked around but didn't see another cabin. I did see a structure that appeared to be a storage shed or maybe a garage of some sort. I walked in that direction. When I opened the door, I found an empty space that appeared to have been used to store a vehicle, but I heard pounding. I followed the sound toward the back of the room, where I found a door. I opened the door and gasped. "Houston," I called out as I hurried forward and knelt down on the dirt floor. "I'm sorry this is going to hurt," I said as I ripped the tape off the mouth of the dark-haired girl from my dreams.

She flinched but didn't cry out when I pulled the tape free.

"Where are the others?" I asked as Houston, Jake, and Dani came into the room from behind me.

"Gone." She began to sob. "You just missed them."

Chapter 7

By the following day, Bella had been returned to her parents, and we had part of the story. According to Bella, she'd been walking home from her after-school piano lesson when someone grabbed her from behind. The person who grabbed her put a hand firmly over her mouth, preventing her from calling out. A large man wearing a ski mask forced her into a van. Someone else drove, but she never saw who that someone was. Bella told Houston that she struggled at first but eventually felt a prick in her neck, and the next thing she knew, she was lying on a filthy mattress in a small cold room with another girl, who identified herself as Lily. She wasn't sure how long they were in the first room before the man with the ski mask came for them. He taped their mouths, tied their wrists, and forced them into the back of a truck with a camper shell.

She said that after they were forced into the truck, they drove for quite a while. Maybe a few hours, although she was terrified, and she didn't really have a real concept of the passage of time. Eventually, they parked. After she was removed from the truck, the man with the ski mask and the old woman, she later learned was called Fran, brought her to the shed where I'd found her via snowmobile. After she was locked up, the man with the ski mask must have gone to fetch Lily and the boy since Lily was tossed in the room at some point later that same evening.

Bella described her captor as a large man with large hands. As she'd mentioned, he wore a ski mask, so she couldn't see his face, but he was a tall man with broad shoulders, who reminded her of the Hulk. During the two instances when they were together, he never spoke, so she didn't have any idea whether or not he had an accent.

She said that hours after she was brought to the cold, windowless room at the end of the snowmobile ride, the old woman had come in with food. Bella shared with Houston that she hadn't wanted to eat, but Lily had convinced her it was important that they kept up their strength, so they could escape.

Bella reported that the old woman who brought the food never stayed and never spoke. She shared that Lily had been calling her Fran, but she didn't know with any certainty if that was her real name.

Houston asked about the boy who'd been mentioned earlier. Bella shared that he appeared to be around fifteen, but she didn't know his age for sure. The boy was large in stature and never spoke or interacted with her directly. She said he mostly just lurked in the background whenever the old woman came with the food.

Bella and Lily had talked during their time together. Bella reported that Lily had been kind and tried to keep her mind off what was going on. Neither girl knew why they'd been taken. They weren't beaten or sexually assaulted. They were simply held. Bella did share that Lily had mentioned that after she was kidnapped, she'd overheard a man speaking to another man from the other side of the door of the first bedroom she was held in. She didn't know if it had been the man with the ski mask speaking or someone else, but she did hear someone make a comment about needing three before the delivery date. Three *what* she wasn't sure of, but she suspected it was three girls.

Houston was going to check into things, but we both agreed that needing three before delivery sounded like a human trafficking sort of thing. Coupled with the fact that the girls were taken but otherwise uninjured, the human trafficking angle made more sense than a serial killer or pedophile trying to get his jollies.

Bella was obviously shaken by the whole experience, and Houston didn't want to push, but he convinced her parents to allow law enforcement in Tok to do a follow-up interview the next day. Apparently, Lily and Bella had heard the chopper earlier in the day and had been hoping to be rescued. Of course, Dani hadn't been able to land in the immediate vicinity, so the actual rescue had been delayed.

The old woman had come in for Lily shortly after the chopper passed, and then Bella heard the snowmobile start up. She knew the snowmobile could accommodate three passengers since there had been three of them when they arrived, so she suspected that the old woman and the boy had taken Lily and planned to meet up with the man with the ski mask somewhere. She also suspected they had chosen Lily over her since she'd been with them longer.

Bella didn't know where they'd been heading before their progress was interrupted by the chopper, but Lily had mentioned that it seemed like they had a specific destination in mind.

"So, what's the plan at this point?" Harley asked as I brought him up to speed during a phone call that had already lasted almost two hours.

"I'm not sure. Houston is going to try to figure out where they're going. The man with the ski mask and his cohorts still have Lily, and he suspects that if the man with the ski mask is supposed to deliver three girls to whoever he's arranged to meet up with, two more will be taken. Based on the location of the two abductions and the location of the cabin where we found them earlier today, it seems apparent they're moving north."

"It does seem that way. Were you able to get any sleep last night?"

"Actually, I slept through the night. I still don't know who I've been channeling, but whoever it is seemed to take the night off. We asked Bella if there was anyone else at the cabin other than the old woman and the teenage boy, and she said not as far as she knew. Assuming the man with the ski mask wasn't on the premises, which is what Bella believed to be true, I must have been inside the head of the teenage boy. It's odd that he lurked in the background and never spoke. I almost wonder if he might be mentally challenged. My experience with being inside his head, assuming it's him that I'm connected with, can best be described as being inside the head of someone without a lot of thoughts or feelings of their own. Usually, when I'm in someone's head, I can hear a lot of internal chatter, if you know what I mean."

"I do know what you mean, and it is odd that whoever you're connecting with isn't trying to speak to you a bit more directly. I guess the boy might be intentionally blocking his thoughts. If this man with the ski mask is using the old woman and the boy to help him kidnap these girls, I guess it makes sense that he'd use people who are easily controlled."

"I guess."

"If the person you're connecting with is this boy, do you think he even knows you're lurking around in his head?" Harley asked.

I paused to consider this. "I'm not sure. Maybe. In a way, it makes no sense that he'd follow the old woman when she goes to feed the girls. He doesn't seem to be helping in any way. Even when there were two girls, she carried both bowls, and she fished the key out of her pocket and opened the door. Doesn't it seem that if she had this person following her, she'd ask him to hold the bowls while she handled the door?"

"I guess that would make sense."

"It's almost as if the old woman isn't aware of this boy's presence, but that doesn't make sense. She must know he's there. I mean, she'd have to be blind for her not to notice him following her."

"Maybe she is blind."

I shook my head even though Harley couldn't see me. "No. She gets around strange places too well to be blind."

"What if the cabins from your dreams aren't strange to her? What if the man and the old woman have done this before? Perhaps many times. Maybe the cabins are actually places she's comfortable moving around in."

"Don't you think that if this man had done this before, Houston would have found other missing girls?"

"Was he looking for other missing girls? Girls who might have gone missing months or even years ago, with no physical trait limitations?"

"No, I guess not," I admitted. "I suppose that might be something to look into, assuming Houston hasn't already done so. If the cabins are hideouts along a route the man with the ski mask and the old woman with the food have traveled before, she might be able to get around even if she is blind. Or maybe Fran isn't blind. Maybe she just has severely limited sight. Maybe she has cataracts that aren't bad enough to cause her to be unable to see forms and images that are right in front of her but are bad enough so that she can't see anything not directly in front of her face. That might allow her to move around carefully, but it might prevent her from noticing that the boy is following her if he keeps his distance."

I made a mental note to ask Houston about other missing girls. It seemed that if the cabins used were seasonal cabins, then the man must take and transport these girls during the winter when they were closed up.

"So why do you think he's following her but not offering to help?" Harley asked after a brief pause.

"Maybe he doesn't want her to know he's there," I answered. "Maybe he's fascinated with the girls and wants to take a peek when the old woman feeds them but knows the old woman will be angry if he shows too much interest."

"I suppose that could be the case. If the boy is fifteen, he's likely to be interested in the girls even if he is developmentally delayed or physically impaired in some way."

"Or," I offered an alternative, "maybe he actually does know I'm in his head and is trying to show me what I need to know to help. Maybe he feels bad for the girls. Maybe he isn't a willing participant in whatever is going on."

"If that were true, don't you think he would have looked outside so you could see where they were or even jotted down a note for you to read through his eyes?"

"I don't know. I guess all we can do at this point is to speculate about what might be going on. I guess we'll need to catch up with this odd group of kidnappers and ask the boy how he's involved."

"I have faith that you'll do just that," Harley encouraged. "The Harmony Carson I know always closes the case."

I smiled. That wasn't necessarily true, but I appreciated the vote of confidence.

"So, how is the movie going?" I asked, changing the subject.

"It's going well. I think we're actually ahead of schedule."

"That's great. How's Brando doing?"

"He's doing really well. The cast and crew love him. If I can't be with him, someone always volunteers. He's actually spent very little time inside the motorhome by himself."

"That's great, Harley. I'm glad everything is working out for you."

"Well, maybe not everything," he said.

"Oh? What's wrong?" I could sense that Harley was irritated more than anything else.

"My agent decided that it would be a good idea to leak the news that my costar and I have been engaged in a steamy affair while on location. Nothing could be further from the truth. Loretta and I are friends.

We've worked together before, so I guess you could say we are good friends. But only friends."

"Loretta? Are you working with Loretta London?"

"Yeah. I thought I told you that."

I pictured the absolutely stunning redhead in my mind. "No. I don't think you mentioned that. How does Loretta feel about the publicity stunt?"

"Actually, she's fine with it. She told me that having her name linked with mine can only help her career and even suggested that maybe we might want to play up the rumor with public displays of affection."

I wrinkled my nose. "Are you going to do it? Publically pretend to date this woman?"

"Absolutely not. I already have an undeserved reputation as a player that I've been trying to unwind. Being seen with Loretta off-screen is only going to perpetuate a stereotype I'd love to leave behind."

"It seems to me that this isn't the first time you've been encouraged to fake an affair with a costar."

"It's not." He let out a long sigh. "I enjoy acting, but I'm really over all the drama that seems to go with it. I'm going to finish this movie, but then I think I'm going to take a long look at my life and my future."

"I suppose that's a good thing to do every now and again even if you aren't Harley Medford Superstar."

"I guess." He paused and then changed the subject. "How are things going at the shelter?"

I filled him in on everything that had been going on, including the kittens who had literally been abandoned on our doorstep. Like me, he was glad they had been dumped there and not somewhere isolated where no one would have found them, but also like me, he wished whoever had abandoned them would have done so during business hours. We continued to chat for another twenty minutes or so, but he eventually informed me that he needed to head out for his afternoon shoot. I said my goodbyes and assured him that, while we all missed him, we'd make sure everything was taken care of during his absence.

After I hung up with Harley, I grabbed my rifle and took my pack out for a walk. It was twilight, although we still had some time until the well-worn path would be difficult to navigate, so we set out for a brisk walk to the lake and back. I'd been noticing cougar tracks in the snow the past few days, so I made sure to keep the dogs close. Once we'd returned from our walk, I headed to the barn to clean stalls and cages. Between my shifts at Neverland, my work as a search-and-rescue volunteer, my volunteer shifts at the shelter, and the menagerie of animals I cared for on a daily basis, I had very little free time, and yet I really did love everything about my life and wouldn't change a thing.

After I was finished in the barn, I headed back to the house to make dinner and maybe read a few chapters of the book I'd been working on for weeks now but couldn't seem to find the time to finish. By the time bedtime rolled around, I was exhausted. I really hoped I'd get another full night's sleep, but the night I hoped for and the night I had, were two entirely different things.

Chapter 8

Tonight's dream was similar to the dreams I'd been having the past couple of weeks. The cabin was a new one, yet it was similar to the others, although it seemed to be even more rustic than the others had been. The bricks backing the old woodstove were chipped and stained, and I didn't notice any sort of fireplace other than an old woodstove that seemed to be doing double duty heating the cabin and heating the food in the cast iron pot.

The old woman wore the same dress she'd worn during every other dream. I hadn't thought to ask Bella if the old woman actually wore the same gray dress every day or if the dress was simply an effect of the dream. I supposed it didn't matter, but I did have to admit I was curious.

As with the other cabins I'd dreamed about, the windows were boarded, so there was no way to determine either the location or time of day, but I suspected that this cabin, like the others, was tucked away well off the beaten path.

As with all the other dreams I'd had, once the old woman dished up the food, she'd headed down a long dark hallway, which after the discovery of the last cabin the girls had been held in, I now knew was a representation of a journey and not an actual hallway. In the second cabin, the old woman would have had to go outside to deliver the food. I wondered why the image I'd seen was a hallway and not the actual landscape she traveled through. I suspected I was viewing a memory and not a live event given the time of day when the dreams occurred, so perhaps the person I was channeling did some editing before showing me what it was he wanted to share. I know that sounded crazy, but as far as I was concerned, this whole thing was crazy.

Tonight, the old woman had two bowls of soup or stew. I hadn't dreamed last night, so I supposed that at some point between yesterday morning when the old woman and the boy had fled with Lily, they'd met up with the man in the ski mask, who'd taken a girl to replace Bella, and they'd found a new place to hole up. I wasn't sure they'd stay where they were given the fact that the man with the ski mask must know that law enforcement was on his trail, but I hoped they'd stay put long enough for us to catch up with them.

In addition to Lily, there was a girl with dark hair and a similar physical appearance and age as Bella. If this man was kidnapping girls to sell, I wondered if he had specific orders to fill in terms of age and overall appearance. I supposed that could be the case, but there was no way to know for sure at this point.

The new girl was terrified, crying as she cowered in the corner. I could see that Lily was doing the best she could to mediate the situation by both calming the girl and offering her thanks to Fran. I wondered if that was intentional. Maybe she realized that trying to make friends with her captors afforded her the best chance for escape.

Again, whoever I was channeling seemed to be lurking in the background. The old woman with the food never acknowledged that anyone was behind her, but tonight, I noticed that Lily glanced at something or someone beyond the old woman and smiled. Had it been the boy and not the old woman who Lily had been smiling at during the last couple of dreams? Had she decided that coaxing the boy into helping her was most likely her best bet? Had the boy decided he would help her? Was that the reason he'd let me into his head? So many questions and not enough answers, but I knew that if I was going to help these girls, I needed to do my best during these brief dreams to see everything there was to see.

Now that I knew what was going on, I could better control what I saw. At least to a degree. I still had no idea if the old woman with the food had traveled down an actual hallway after dishing up whatever was in the pot on the old woodstove or if she'd ventured outside to an outbuilding as she had at the last cabin the group had stayed in. The windows were boarded, so I couldn't see out, and I hadn't actually noticed a door, but knew there was one. Based on prior dreams, I knew that once the old woman delivered the food and closed the bedroom door, I'd wake up. My time there tonight was over, but I was determined to try to communicate with whoever's head I was in during my next dream.

As predicted, I woke once the food was delivered, and the bedroom door had closed. I hated to wake Houston, but if a new girl had been taken, time was of the essence, so I punched in his number and waited.

"Harmony?" He must have sat up or looked at the clock or something at this point because his next words were a lot less groggy. "You had another dream."

"I did. The same as the others, but there was a new cabin with a new girl. Dark hair, with similar features and age as Bella."

"Okay. I'm going to grab my things, and I'll be over. You can walk me through everything. I'll do a search for missing persons within a hundred-mile radius and see what I come up with. Put the coffee on. I have a feeling it's going to be a long day."

After I hung up with Houston, I slipped out of bed and pulled my robe on. I let the dogs out, started the fire, and put on a pot of coffee. Once the dogs came back from their bathroom break, I headed into the bathroom for a shower. I'd just returned to the main room after getting dressed and drying my hair when Houston pulled up.

"Emily Deerchild," he said after handing me his computer bag so he could return to his truck for the maps and files he'd brought.

"Emily Deerchild?" I asked. "Is that the new victim?"

He nodded as he entered the cabin and set everything in his arms on the table. "Twelve years old, brown hair, blue eyes. Emily was last seen leaving school yesterday afternoon."

"This guy didn't waste any time replacing Bella."

Houston unzipped his computer bag, slipping the laptop out and plugging it in. "If I had to bet, he'd originally planned to kidnap girl number three yesterday. If Lily was correct when she told Bella that the man with the ski mask needed three girls, he would have been finishing up and heading toward the meeting place, but now that he's lost Bella, he's going to need a third. I suspect he may take a third girl as early as today. Maybe tomorrow, depending on his timeline for delivery."

"So we need to track these girls down ASAP."

"Exactly."

I handed Houston a mug of coffee. "Okay. So where do we start?"

Houston looked at me. "I know that to this point, you've been having these visions while you're sleeping. They seem to come to you rather than you conjuring them up. I also know that when a rescue is involved, you sit and focus on the victim and that it's your intent that initiates the contact. Do you think that if you tried, you'd be able to contact the person whose mind you've been lurking in?"

I hesitated. Even the act of being a witness and not an instigator had left me feeling drained and headachy. Initiating contact was always challenging, and each time I did it, I felt like it stripped something away from me. I knew that even if I could find a way to get inside the head of the individual I'd been channeling, it was going to take more out of me than I was sure I had to give.

"Yes," I eventually answered. "I think I know enough now to try." I looked toward the sofa where Moose was curled up asleep. I was going to need him for sure. "Bella gave you a description of the boy we think I've been connecting with. I'm going to settle in with Moose, and you are going to slowly describe him to me while I focus."

"Okay. Whatever you need," Houston said.

I drank half my mug of coffee before heading to the sofa. I sat down and pulled Moose into my lap. Moose was not a lap cat and would often squirm away when I tried to cuddle with him, but today he seemed to know we had work to do since he snuggled in and began to purr. I closed my eyes and focused on the cabin I'd seen in my dreams just a few hours ago. I opened my mind and willed my consciousness to merge with the host who'd found me so many times in the last two weeks.

"Bella described the boy as being around fifteen. Husky build. Tall. Strong looking," Houston began.

I tried to create an image in my mind.

"Dark hair. Longish. Maybe shoulder length. Dark eyes that appeared sympathetic."

Houston paused, and I focused in.

"Quiet. Never speaks. Keeps his distance and seems to lurk in the shadows," Houston continued. It sounded like he was reading from his notes and probably was. "Bella hadn't been with him long enough to have forged an impression of his personality or intention, but Lily had told her that he seemed kind. Bella wasn't sure if this was accurate. If he was really kind, she reasoned, he would have found a way to help them when it was just them and the old woman." I could sense Houston looking up from his notes. "I guess the man with the ski mask might have conditioned him to do what he was told even when he wasn't around."

My memory of the dream I'd had last night was vivid. When I arrived in the mind of the person I assumed was the boy this time, the cabin was dark. Totally dark. Of course, it was still totally dark outside, so perhaps I'd managed to connect with the boy in real-time. If I had, I might be able to use that connection to figure out where they were. I looked around, but it was totally dark, so I really couldn't see a thing. I could feel the person whose mind I shared awaken. As his mind settled into an alert state, I noticed him moving toward the stove.

"This isn't a wood stove," I said as I got a closer look. "It's one of those stoves that works on a generator."

"A generator?"

I nodded. "I noticed last night during my dream that the cabin didn't seem to have a fireplace but I didn't realize that the stove didn't burn wood either."

"Maybe the man with the ski mask learned his lesson about wood smoke."

"Yeah," I agreed. That did seem likely.

"What else are you noticing?" Houston asked.

I paused and continued to look around. I felt more in control of my thoughts and movements than I did when I was the observer during my dream state. "The old woman is awake. She's sitting next to the stove. I suppose it must be putting off some heat since she seemed to be cooking on it in my dream. I can't know for sure, but I'm guessing the cabin is either a forest service cabin like the one we found the group using two days ago, or it might be a private fishing and hunting cabin. It's barren, but it does seem to have a generator, so that makes me think it might be privately owned."

"What is the boy whose mind you're visiting doing?" Houston asked.

"It feels like he's just sitting where he slept. When I first entered his mind, I believe he was sleeping. He appears to be fully alert now, but I haven't sensed that he's moved." I took a breath. "I suppose he senses me and is trying to make sense of the whole thing."

"Any clue at all as to where the cabin might be located?"

I looked around and tried to hone in on something, but it was too dark. I really needed someone to light one of the oil lamps. I remember seeing a lamp on the table from my previous visit, so I focused all my attention on it, hoping the boy would understand what I wanted him to do. At first, he didn't move, but after a bit, I could sense movement.

"He's moving around now," I said. "I'm focusing on the lamp. It's dark, so all I can see are outlines of images."

I remembered from my dream last night that the walls were bare, the furniture sparse and very well used. The kitchen where the old woman had gone for the spoons had shelves with dishware. Not a lot of it and not matched, but it looked like the cabin was outfitted for cooking. The walls were log, the floor was natural pine with deep scratches. There was a rug toward the center of the room. It looked like it had been green at one time but had turned gray due most likely to wear and dirt.

I smiled as the lantern was lit, and the room came into view. It was a subdued view, but I could see enough to get a feel for things. The first thing I noticed was a hallway. It was an actual hallway, not just a representation. I couldn't see how far it went, but the hallway looked to have several rooms off it rather than only the bathroom the previous cabin had. As I noticed each of these features, I described them to Houston.

"I'm going to try to deepen my connection. Don't talk to me for the next few minutes, and don't interrupt me. I might call out, or I might start to cry, but just let me do what I need to do."

"Okay," Houston said. I could hear the reluctance in his voice, but he'd worked with me before as I'd made painful connections, so by this point, I supposed he knew the drill.

As I relaxed and opened my mind, the first thing I noticed was fear. Fear of what I wasn't sure, but I did know that the fear belonged to the boy. I supposed he might be afraid of the man who held them captive. Or his fear might have been for the girls who the boy I was channeling seemed to want to help. Just because this boy appeared to be helping the man didn't mean that he wasn't as much a victim as the girls he was watching were.

"Are you there?" I thought, speaking silently to the person whose mind I'd connected with. "I can feel your pain. Your concern for the girls. I want to help."

The harder I focused, the more sure I was that my head was literally going to explode. The pain had grown quite intense, but still, I focused harder.

"I know you're scared, but I need you to help me," I said in my mind. "I can't help Lily if I don't know where she is. I know you want to help her."

Even as I said the words, I knew they had no meaning for the boy. Bella said that the boy never spoke. Maybe he was deaf. If he was deaf and had never been taught to speak or read, the words would have no meaning. I decided to try to play out my words in my mind. I began by creating an image of Lily in my mind. Suddenly I felt an outpouring of love for the blond-haired girl who'd been with them about two weeks now. I tapped into a memory where she'd made eye contact and smiled at him. She'd seen him and acknowledged his presence when he seemed to be invisible to everyone else. It was at that moment that he'd decided to help her. It was in that moment that he'd begun letting me in.

I focused harder. I knew speaking to the boy with words wouldn't work, so instead, I imagined a scene where he found a flashlight and went outside. I focused intently on the door. I showed him that if he did this for me, then men would come who would help Lily escape. I imagined Lily being happy when she was rescued. I imagined her being grateful to him. I even imagined her giving him a hug.

I could sense that the boy had gotten up. He didn't say anything to the old woman who was still sitting quietly in the chair by the stove as he grabbed an oil lamp from the table, lit it, and headed toward the door. The old woman didn't say anything. I actually think she might have been asleep in the chair. The boy hesitated at the door. Again, I focused on a scene where the boy opened the door, and Lily was saved.

The boy opened the door and stepped outside. I looked around frantically. I could feel his fear, but I could also sense his resolve. He walked toward an outbuilding, which I realized must be an outhouse. I supposed that was a good idea. If the old woman woke and noticed that he was outdoors, she wouldn't give a second thought about him using the facilities so early in the morning.

Luckily, it was a clear night, and there was light from the stars and moon. When the boy had first stepped out, I noticed that the ground was covered with snow. Not surprising. By this point in the winter, most of the state was covered in snow. As the boy slowly walked toward the outbuilding, I looked around as quickly as I could. There were trees growing densely in every direction, so it was difficult to get a lay of the land, but I did notice a tall mountain in the distance that had a high enough summit to be seen beyond the trees.

"Bearpaw Peak," I said aloud.

I didn't mean to break the connection, but that was exactly what happened. One minute I was connected with the boy, and the next, he was gone. I opened my eyes.

"Did you see something?" Houston asked.

"The boy is in love with Lily. He's scared. I suppose he's afraid of the man with the ski mask, but he wants to help her, so he's willing to take small risks. He allowed me to come along as he went outside. The cabin is in a deep forest surrounded by trees, but I could see Bearpaw Peak to the west." I got up and walked over to the table. I rolled out a map. I pointed to a wilderness area, about one hundred and fifty miles away, which would take a good four hours to reach by road given the weather. "I think they're holed up right about here."

"That's only about sixty miles from where Emily was taken, so that part fits."

I turned and looked out the window. "We need to go have a look around." I turned back toward the map. "There's a town here." I pointed to Huntsville, the town I'd visited with a mysterious man. A man who filtered in and out of my life.

"That's where you went with Shredder the first Christmas I was here," Houston said.

"That's right," I said. "I'll call Jake and tell him I need a few days off. I'll call Serena and make sure she's okay at the shelter. And then I'll call Justine and see if she can come and stay at my place and take care of the animals." I looked at the clock. "The sun will rise in three and a half hours. I can be ready in less than two. We should hit the road as soon as we can. We should have around six hours of daylight today. We'll need every one of them."

Houston nodded. "Okay. I'll head back to my place and pack a bag. I'll let my men know what I'm doing, and then I'll come back for you."

"Bring any survival supplies you have. The road between here and the town where we're heading is rustic. The odds of getting stuck are actually pretty good." I paused to consider things. "We should bring our snowmobiles too. We'll probably need them. I can load mine onto your trailer. If you want to bring Kojak, I'll bring Yukon. You have an extended cab, so they can ride in the back seat. You never know when an experienced search-and-rescue dog might come in handy."

Taking the road we planned to travel could be tricky during the winter, but Houston had a big four-wheel-drive truck with a long bed, custom wheels, and tires built for backwoods travel, tow bar, winch, and spotlights for additional illumination. If there was a truck that was made for a trip like this, it was Houston's.

"By the time we arrive in town, we'll have less than three hours of daylight left. We'll do what we can, spend the night, assuming we don't find them right away, and then continue our search the following day."

"Should we ask Dani about using the chopper?"

I shook my head. "She has a charter today." I glanced at the clock. "She's actually already in the air. She'll be out of town until tomorrow afternoon. I suppose we can call her to come up when she gets back if we decide her presence would be useful. Based on what I saw in my vision, there's a lot of tree cover in the area where the cabin is located, and unless they decide to use wood for the stove rather than the generator, we'll never find them. We wouldn't have found them the last time if we hadn't caught a break by following the trail from the smoke." I got up and began tidying up the kitchen. "I wish we could use the chopper, but I think this rescue mission is going to need to be accomplished the hard way."

"You mean by wandering around in subfreezing temperatures looking for a needle in a haystack."

"Exactly."

Chapter 9

By the time Houston returned, I'd packed my bags, walked the dogs, fed and provided fresh water to the animals in the barn, and made all my calls. Jake assured me he had things handled at Neverland and made me promise to check in with him. Serena was fine at the shelter, and Justine was fine to stay at my place and look after the kids. Jake offered to check in with her as well. Denali was a protective dog, so I couldn't ask just anyone to stay at the cabin, but he loved both Justine and Jake, so I was sure they'd be just fine.

The road heading north out of Rescue was desolate. There was one small waystation with a bar and a gas station about eighty miles north, and then there's nothing until you hit Huntsville, the small town where Houston and I planned to stay. Although

Houston had filled his tank before we'd left Rescue, there was an unwritten Alaskan law that basically stated that when traveling in this part of the state, you never passed up a chance to top off your tank.

"There's a truck stop on the map that's about thirty minutes from here. Should we stop?" Houston asked after we'd been driving for a while."

"We should. We'll top off the tank, grab some coffee, and use the restrooms. If you're hungry, grab a snack. While it appears that the next little town isn't all that far down the road, it's a rough road to travel in the winter, and you never know what might happen along the way."

Houston nodded. "Okay. We'll stop. I could use a refill of coffee and a chance to stretch my legs." He looked into the back seat where both dogs were riding. "I think the dogs would appreciate the chance to stretch their legs as well."

The truck stop was really little more than a bar, gas station, and mini-mart. The owner lived in an apartment over the bar and the only employee, other than the owner, lived in a wilderness cabin not far away. I headed toward the ladies' room while Houston topped off the tank. I figured we could both take the dogs for a quick walk and refill our coffee before continuing.

"By the way," I said after we'd let the dogs out and headed across the dirt lot. "Did you have a chance to do a search for other missing girls in either Alaska or Canada?"

"I did. I didn't find any other girls who went missing in Alaska during the last year, but I did find three girls in Canada who were taken three years ago. They never did turn up."

I really, really hated to hear that.

"It occurred to me that our kidnapper might work in different areas, so I searched other states and found two girls missing from Oregon and one from Washington State last winter. All were either eleven or twelve, and none were ever seen again."

"Sounds like this guy has a contract to kidnap these girls, but he moves around so as not to be easily caught. Anything before that?" I asked as we returned to the truck and piled in.

"I didn't find any missing girls from the Pacific Northwest, Western Canada, or Alaska prior to three years ago, but I didn't have a lot of time to look. I did find an eleven-year-old boy named Jeremy Taylor from North Pole, Alaska, who seems to have gone missing four years ago. Well, sort of."

"What do you mean by sort of?"

"I'm not absolutely sure the boy is actually missing. The report I read stated that the eleven-year-old girl who lived next door to Jeremy told her parents that she was afraid something had happened to him. I guess she used to see him on a daily basis, and then all of a sudden, he was gone. The girl's parents called the police, who spoke to the boy's father. Jeremy's father told the police officer who interviewed him that Jeremy was simply visiting an uncle. The police officer had no reason to question his statement, but he made a note in the file that something seemed off."

"If Jeremy had been kidnapped, why would his father lie?" I asked as Houston pulled onto the highway. "Besides, a boy doesn't necessarily fit the pattern of the missing girls you've identified."

"That's true, but I did some checking, and Jeremy never did return to North Pole. The whole thing feels off to me."

"So, you think Jeremy is the fifteen-year-old boy Bella told us about, and I've supposedly been connecting with?"

"Maybe. According to what I could find, Jeremy seems to share a similar coloring and build as the boy Bella described. I also found it interesting that Jeremy was born deaf."

"That has to be him. I've suspected that it might be possible the person I've been connecting with is deaf. And if Jeremy is the boy I've been channeling, being deaf might explain why the kidnapper is able to control him so easily. Did you find any other information about the boy?"

"Jeremy's mother died when he was an infant. He was raised by an abusive man who didn't think it was worth the time and effort it would take to send a deaf child to school, so he basically just made use of his height and strength to assist him with his lumber company. Based on information gained from the interviews that were conducted by the police at the time of his disappearance, it seems that Jeremy's father treated him more like an object than a person.

He was never able to have friends, and he never seemed to learn how to interact with others."

I thought about the boy I'd connected with. It had been hard to read his thoughts since he didn't "think" in words, but he didn't seem like the sort of person who would kill someone. I did wonder how he'd gotten hooked up with the man with the ski mask. Had he been kidnapped, or had he gone with him willingly in an effort to escape his abusive father?

"So, as far as you know, Jeremy had no friends?" I verified, even though Houston had just said as much.

"None, except for Laura, the girl who lived next door and reported him as missing in the first place. According to Laura, Jeremy never spoke to her or anyone for that matter. She told the officer who interviewed her that she would sometimes sit with him and talk about her day." Houston sped up a bit as the road flattened out. "Laura shared that even though she knew Jeremy couldn't hear what she was saying, he seemed to enjoy just sitting with her. She also told the investigator that he'd watch her intently as she spoke, and felt that she might have been able to teach him to communicate if they would have had more time together."

"What did Laura look like?"

"Laura was an eleven year old with blond hair at the time of Jeremy's disappearance."

"So maybe Lily reminds him of Laura."

"Maybe."

Jeremy. I rolled the name around in my mind. Perhaps when I next connected with the boy, I'd try out the name and see what sort of response I got. Of course, if Jeremy was deaf and had never been taught words, then he probably had no idea he even had a name. Still, it couldn't hurt to try to connect again. If Lily reminded Jeremy of one of the only people in his life who was ever kind to him, then maybe, just maybe, he'd be willing to do whatever it took to rescue her.

"Do you have a photo of Laura?" I asked.

"I have a photo of her four years ago when she was interviewed. At least, I have a photo in the file which I can access from my laptop."

"The boy I've been connecting with thinks in images and intentions rather than words. I'm going to try to conjure up a picture of Laura in my mind the next time I connect with him and see what happens. If nothing else, his reaction will probably tell us whether or not it's Jeremy who is currently with the girls."

"I'll pull up a photo when we get to the room. Did you have any trouble getting reservations?"

"No. The place has a lot of vacancies at this time of the year. As I indicated I planned to, I booked two rooms for two nights, but the man I spoke to said that if we needed to extend, it wouldn't be a problem."

"I remember that you told me that when you came north with Shredder, the Grizzly Inn was filled to capacity, and you had to share a room."

I nodded. "We did have to share, but it was Christmastime, and the town was bursting with visitors. We just happened to ask about a room shortly after someone had called and canceled, or we wouldn't have gotten the room we had." I found I was actually looking forward to staying at the inn again. I remembered that the place was warm and comfy, and I remembered the food as being excellent.

"I have to admit that I'm starving," Houston said as he sped up just a bit. "Perhaps I should have grabbed something from the little store at the gas station while we were there, as you suggested."

"Yeah. It's going to be a while before we arrive at our destination. The road only gets worse from here. It's a straight shot, which helps, but it's also icy and filled with unseen potholes. The only way to get there in one piece is to take it slow."

I'd only traveled this road a handful of times in my lifetime, but, generally speaking, my memories of this particular stretch of pavement were fond ones. There was the time I'd come with my parents, and we'd happened across a herd of wild caribou just before Christmas. I was sure they were Santa's reindeer. And then, when I came with Shredder three Christmases ago, there was the mystery of the mysterious handoff to keep my mind engaged. I supposed I had felt a certain amount of stress when I'd come with Shredder, but the stress I'd felt then was nothing compared to the stress I felt now, knowing that the lives of innocent children were at stake.

"Are you okay?" Houston asked. "You keep grimacing and rubbing your head."

"I'm fine." I continued to rub my head. "I guess I'm still feeling the after-effects of my efforts to connect with the boy this morning, but I'll be fine." I looked out the window as the snowy landscape sped past. "I've always enjoyed this drive."

"It's beautiful," he agreed.

"Have you thought about how we're going to proceed once we reach the inn?"

He hesitated. "The only advantage we seem to have is your connection with the boy. I did pull up all sorts of maps: topographical maps, maps of seasonal cabins, roads, snowmobile trails, even dog sled routes. I suppose that will give us a place to search, but I really think our best bet is if you can connect with him again. Maybe you can convince this boy to really work with us to get those girls to safety. At the very least, maybe you can confirm that the group is still in the same cabin where they were this morning."

"Yeah." I cringed as a pain that felt like a knife sliced through my brain. "Connecting will really be the secret to a successful trip."

Houston turned and glanced at me. "I really hate that you have to do this when it's obvious that it causes you so much pain. Maybe we can figure out another way."

"There is no other way. Not without an endless amount of time to look around, which we both know that we don't have. I'll be fine," I assured him.

He didn't look convinced, but he didn't try to talk me out of it either.

Bearpaw Peak could be seen in the distance as we neared the town. We still had a few hours of sunlight left, and I wondered if maybe we shouldn't make use of it while we had it. There's an old road that wasn't maintained but was used by those living in the area. I suspected that with Houston's heavy-duty truck, we could travel at least part of the way down the road for a closer look. I doubted the cabins were accessible by motorized vehicles other than snowmobiles or a Snowcat, of course, but it still seemed that it might be a good use of the light we had to get as close as we were able to before checking in at the inn. I suggested as much to Houston, and he agreed.

"You'll need to tell me where to turn," Houston said.

I paused as I tried to remember exactly where the old service road was located. "The turn is going to be on your left. The road won't have been plowed, but it should be packed down by snowmobiles and local traffic. I'd say the road should appear within the next ten to fifteen minutes, based on our current speed. I'll help you watch for it." I turned around and looked at the dogs, who were sitting up and looking out the windows on either side of the back seat. "You do have tire chains, don't you? Just in case."

"I have chains. Hopefully, we won't need them." He slowed down just a bit, so he wouldn't pass the road. "How's your headache?"

"It's okay," I lied. I narrowed my gaze as I focused on the landscape to the left. The road wasn't a main highway and wouldn't be marked by a sign. If we didn't want to miss it, we were going to have to pay attention.

As the road approached, Houston slowed even more. We made the turn and then followed the road as far as it felt safe, given the condition of the hard-packed snow. Once we'd gone as far as we felt comfortable going without using the tire chains, Houston pulled over and parked. We let the dogs out of the truck, and then we followed them down the road. At this point, the mountain was clearly visible. I tried to get a feel for the cabin's location, based on the angle from which I'd viewed the cabin through the boy's eyes.

"This feels wrong," I said as I looked toward the mountain. "We're looking at the mountain from the south. I feel like the boy looked at the mountain from the north." I paused and looked around. "Once we get to the inn, we'll take a look at the maps." I thought back to what I'd seen. "There's this little gully on the mountain. I assume an avalanche created it at some point. The gully is deep enough that you can really pick it out. It sort of looks like a crooked cross. Based on what I remember, I was looking right at that cross when the boy looked toward the mountain, or when I did through his eyes. I'll have to look at a map to know for sure, but I do seem to remember that the cross is on the northern side of the mountain, which means we'll need to travel north of town."

"Is there a road?" Houston asked.

I laughed. "Yes, if you can call it that. It's going to make the road we just traveled seem like a freshly paved expressway. Still, as long as it doesn't snow, we should be fine. It's actually been pretty dry all week. Once we get lined up, we'll need to take the snowmobiles and continue toward the cabins. We'll want to bring our snowshoes with us as well."

Houston looked toward the sky. "It's getting dark. I guess we should continue to the inn."

"Yeah," I agreed. The short days of winter really did make it hard to get much done when what needed to be accomplished really couldn't be done in the dark.

Houston called the dogs and loaded them into the truck. I settled into the front seat and closed my eyes. My head was already pounding, and I hadn't attempted to connect for a second time as we'd discussed. I probably should have brought Moose with us, but he hated riding in cars, so I supposed I'd have to dig deep and find the strength to do this on my own.

Chapter 10

The Grizzly Inn, which catered to hunters and fishermen during the summer, spring, and fall, was rustic. During December, the inn played host to people who came to the small town looking for the magic of Christmas, but it was mostly empty during the remainder of winter, which meant we had our choice of rooms. I remembered from my trips in the past that all the rooms were nice, so I simply asked for adjoining rooms, each with a fireplace and attached bath.

Houston and I split up after registering. We decided to take a few minutes to wash up and settle in, and then we planned to meet in the lobby, from which we would head out to find a meal. When Shredder and I'd been here, we'd had pizza, which actually sounded really good, providing, of course, that the same little pizza parlor was still around two years later.

I supposed I could simply ask the desk clerk if the little pizza parlor was still around. It would save us a trip if it wasn't.

Once I settled into my room, I laid down on the bed and closed my eyes. I didn't want to fall asleep, but I really did need to find a way to quell the pain in my head. I supposed I should get up and take a couple painkillers. Not the prescription kind that made me drowsy since I still had work to do before I could rest, but the over the counter sort I had tucked away in my bag. Of course, getting up off the bed required effort. Perhaps I'd just lay here for a minute before getting up.

If not for the fact that Yukon jumped up onto the bed just as I was beginning to drift away, I would most likely have done the exact thing I'd vowed not to do. Swinging my legs over to the side of the bed, I grabbed my overnight bag, found the headache medication I'd decided to take, and then headed into the bathroom to splash some cold water on my face and run a brush through my hair. As I considered myself in the mirror, I realized that everyone was right – I really did look awful.

I hadn't thought to bring makeup, so there was no fixing my state of exhaustion by covering it up. I guessed Houston would simply have to deal with the real Harmony Carson during dinner, whether the image I currently projected was the image I wanted to or not.

"I remember this town as being so cheery and festive," I said as we walked through the town toward the pizza parlor the desk clerk had assured me was still there. The fresh air had helped, and I really did feel less groggy. Even my headache was less intense than it had been, but it certainly wasn't gone. "The place feels sort of drab and dreary without the lights and decorations to brighten things up."

"A lot of the businesses are boarded up until the spring, which I guess is true of a lot of towns in Northern Alaska. I suspect the summers are as nice as the holidays are. We just happened to come at the worst time of the year. Still, if it had been summer or the holiday season, we most likely wouldn't have gotten last-minute rooms."

"True," I said as we walked into the pizza parlor to find the place deserted. Even the restaurant felt drab and dreary compared to when I'd been here two years ago. I hoped the food was still good.

After we ordered at the counter, we found a booth near a window and waited for the meat lovers pie to arrive. I shared memories of my trip to the little town two years ago and how this trip compared. Houston shared a similar experience he'd had after visiting a town in Northern Minnesota both during the holidays and during the winter after the holiday. It disappointed me that the town wasn't nearly as enchanting as I remembered, but at least the food was as good as I'd envisioned.

After we ate, we walked back to the inn, where we picked up the truck. We'd decided to head toward the gas station to top off the tank, so we wouldn't have to do it in the morning. We brought the dogs with us and planned to stop somewhere and let them run around before returning to the inn.

Once the truck was fueled and the dogs were exercised, we returned to our rooms. It was decided that Yukon and I would head over to Houston's room through the connecting door since he'd already set up his laptop and laid out the maps he'd brought. The room only held a table where our maps were laid out, a bed, and a small sofa sitting in front of the gas fireplace. I was chilled from our exercise session with the dogs, so I decided to stand in front of the fire before addressing the real reason Yukon and I were here.

"Before I try to connect, let's take a look at the photo of Laura," I said. "I want to have her image firmly in my mind."

Houston pulled up the file on his laptop. I walked across the room, looked at the laptop, and studied the image until I could pull it up in my mind.

"Okay. I'm going to lie down on the bed and try to connect. I'm not certain I can make a connection, but if I can, my main focus will be on confirming that the group is still in the same cabin they were in this morning. I'm not sure how long I'll have. So far, my visits in this boy's mind have been brief and abruptly cut off whether I'm ready to leave or not."

"Just do what you can," Houston said. "Is there anything I can do?"

I looked at him and considered the question. "Normally, I cling to Moose when I undertake a direct connection, but he's not here. Would you lie down next to me? Don't talk to me. Just let me hold your hand."

"Okay," he said, slipping his shoes off.

I lay down on the bed, and Houston lay down next to me. I closed my eyes and focused on an image of the boy Bella had described. I was pretty sure this boy was Jeremy, but I wasn't certain of that, so I focused on his image and not his name. Not that he'd necessarily recognize his name anyway.

At first, I got nothing. Not a feeling. Not a vision. Nothing. I realized that my only chance was to keep at it, so I deepened my focus and tried to block everything else from my mind. Eventually, I was able to pick up a feeling. Fear. In addition to the fear, there was also a deep confusion. I noticed an uncertainty I really couldn't identify. The boy seemed to be resisting my presence, so I changed my focus and tried to visualize Laura. That must have startled him because he let down his guard, and I slipped in. I quickly looked around. I was able to confirm that the cabin the boy was physically occupying was the same one I'd seen earlier that morning. That was something. It was doubtful they'd move overnight, so at least we had a starting point for our search tomorrow.

I looked around the room to see what else I might be able to see. The old woman was sitting in a chair. It was the same chair where she'd been sitting that morning. She wasn't moving, but I supposed she might be asleep. It wasn't late, but it was dark. The cabin was dark with the exception of a single oil lamp. I didn't notice a pot on the stove or evidence of cooking, but perhaps the old woman had already fed the girls and cleaned up.

While I was trying to decide what I wanted to find out from the boy I was channeling, he seemed to look down the hallway. I was hoping he'd go and check on the girls so that I could confirm that they were physically okay and that a third girl hadn't as of yet been taken, but something caused the boy to break the connection, and no matter how hard I tried, I couldn't get it back.

When I opened my eyes, I was lying with my cheek on Houston's chest. He had his arms around me and was hanging on tight. When we'd first laid down, we'd been lying side by side, but I supposed at some point, I probably called out, and he'd tucked me in tight.

I turned my head and looked up at him. My head was pounding, but his smile when our eyes met still took my breath away.

"You're back," he said, loosening his grip just a bit.

I nodded. I was pretty darn comfy and hated to pull away, but we had a job to do, so I sat up, and Houston followed.

"Did you see anything?" he asked after handing me a bottle of water.

I nodded, taking a long drink before I answered. "Not a lot. I wasn't connected long, but I know that they are in the same cabin they were in this morning.

The old woman was sleeping, I think. I'm not a hundred percent sure since she was sitting in the same chair that she was sitting in this morning, but she wasn't moving, so I guess she was sleeping."

"We're you able to see the girls?"

I shook my head. "The boy only let me in briefly, and only after I visualized Laura. I think he was resisting me, but when I pictured her, I think it startled him enough that he let his guard down for a minute, and I slipped in. During my brief time in the boy's mind, he didn't move, so I wasn't able to see the girls. I didn't notice anything that was different from when I peeked in this morning, so I'm going to assume that nothing has changed. Based on his past movements, the man with the ski mask moves them when he takes a new girl, and since they seemed to have stayed put, I'm going to assume that a third girl has not been added to the mix yet."

"He's likely to make his move tomorrow," Houston said.

"I agree. We'll head out in the morning before dawn. The snowmobiles have headlights, and it's supposed to be clear, so we'll have the moonlight to help us. Hopefully, we can get all the way out to where the cabins are located around the time the sun comes up." I flinched as searing pain penetrated my head. "I think I'll call down for some brandy. This headache is worse than most, and I doubt I'll sleep if I can't get rid of it."

"I actually have both brandy and aspirin," Houston said. He got up and crossed to his suitcase.

"I called and spoke to Jake before we left. I asked him what I could bring that might help you once we got started, and he said brandy and aspirin."

I forced a smile. "Thank you. I appreciate that you're looking out for me. I took an over the counter pain medication earlier, but I wouldn't say no to brandy."

Once I drank the first glass of brandy, Houston poured me a second glass, and then we headed toward the table where the maps were laid out. I pointed to the place on the mountain where I was sure the cross left by an avalanche existed, and Houston overlaid the map of the seasonal cabins in the area. The cabins weren't clustered quite as neatly as we hoped they'd be, but after taking into account things such as access to the road and the tree canopy, we settled on a search area. We weren't sure how long it would take to make the drive and then the eventual snowmobile ride, so we decided to get up at six, and if we needed to wait for sunlight at any point, we'd simply stop and take a break.

We discussed taking the dogs. Both dogs were comfortable riding along as a passenger on the two-man snowmobiles. They'd both been trained as search-and-rescue dogs, and in snow country, they had the ability to settle onto the loud machines, which was a must. After a bit of discussion, we decided to take them. I wasn't sure we'd need them, but I did know that they'd prefer to go with us rather than staying in the room, and their ability to sniff out a trail might come in handy once we reached the search grid we were heading toward.

Of course, all of this would be for naught if the group had decided to move. I really had no way of knowing what sort of plans the man with the ski mask might have, but I did find myself saying a little prayer that even if he planned to move, he'd wait until after we had the chance to catch up with them.

Chapter 11

When I woke the following morning, I was surprised to find that I'd slept through the night. I was happy to have had the added sleep but afraid that the reason I hadn't had the dream might be due to the fact that the boy had been spooked by my showing up in his mind uninvited. I had to wonder if maybe he'd found a way to block me. I'd hoped that by bringing Laura to mind, I would be able to convince him to trust me, but I supposed that now that I'd had a chance to think about it, the image of Laura I conjured in our shared thoughts might simply have sent him running.

I didn't suppose second-guessing myself at this point would do any good. All I could do was continue with the plan Houston and I had come up with and hope that it wasn't too late to rescue the girls and catch the man who'd taken them. I wondered where the man with the ski mask went after he'd stashed the old woman, the girls he'd kidnapped, and the boy in the cabins I'd experienced over the past two weeks. Did he have a place to stay, or did he simply head into town and rent out a room?

I could hear Houston moving around in the adjoining room. It was still pitch black outside, but I knew, based on the readout on the bedside clock, that I needed to get up and going as well. Since I knew we'd be out in the elements for most of the day, I piled on layers of clothing. I began with thermal underwear and worked out from there with a lightweight yet waterproof layer, which I topped with ski pants and a heavy sweater. Once we arrived at our destination, I would add my snowmobile jacket, heavy gloves, snow boots, and a hat. For now, I simply piled my outerwear on the bed.

I knew that Yukon would need to go out, and he would need to be fed as well. I wasn't sure what sort of plan Houston had for the dogs, so I knocked on the adjoining door. When he answered, I could see that he was dressed much as I was, although the dampness of his hair led me to believe he'd taken the time to shower, which I hadn't. Of course, his hair would dry quickly, while my long thick hair would take quite a while, even with an electric hair dryer, and I knew that at this moment, getting on the road was more important than looking my best.

"Should we take the dogs out for a bathroom run and then feed them before we head out?" I asked.

"The gas station on the edge of town is open and will have coffee," he said. "I thought we'd stop there, let the dogs run around, and then feed them while we have our coffee. The stop shouldn't take long, but on cold mornings such as this, I really need hot coffee to get my blood pumping."

"I'm glad you said that. I was actually thinking the same thing." I glanced behind me. "I think I have everything I need."

"Okay. Let's load up the truck and head out."

I grabbed my outerwear, and Houston grabbed his. We, and the dogs, headed down the empty hallway to the lobby, where we accessed the exterior door and exited into the parking lot. I could see that Houston had already made at least one trip down to the truck since the maps we were looking at last night were rolled up and stashed behind the back seat.

I glanced up into the starlit sky. Not a cloud in sight. I really, really hoped the weather held. There weren't many things more miserable and potentially dangerous than snowmobiling when it was snowing heavily. Besides, given the dry conditions we'd had this past week, the snowmobile tracks made by the man with the ski mask and the group he was traveling with should still be evident once we made our way closer to the grouping of cabins we were heading toward. At least they should be evident if we were correct in our assumptions.

Once Yukon and Kojak had run around a bit and woofed down a healthy breakfast, the four of us resumed our journey. The road north out of town was only a gravel road, which, even when there wasn't ice and snow to consider, provided a bumpy and often perilous journey. I knew that as long as Houston took it slow and didn't lose his concentration, we should be fine, but even with my confidence in his driving ability, for some reason, I couldn't quite relax.

"Did you dream last night?" he asked after we were underway.

"No." I paused and looked out the window. "I haven't decided if I should be worried about that. I think the boy might be feeling overwhelmed now that I'm a much more active participant in his thoughts. I think he might be intentionally blocking me."

"Can he do that?"

"Sure. If the boy knows what's going on, which I'm certain he does. The other alternative is that the dreams I've been having are linked to his dreams and based on his memories of recent events. That actually makes sense now that we know for sure that he's here in Alaska and in the same time zone as me. If I'm having the dreams at three a.m., he is most likely asleep at that time of the day as well."

"So an alternative to his intentionally blocking you is that he didn't sleep."

I took a sip of my now tepid coffee. "Exactly." I thought back to our encounter. "He seemed really stressed when I connected with him yesterday. That may be because I initiated the contact and was intentionally trying to communicate with him, and he didn't know what to do with that, but there might also be something more going on. Maybe the group is nearing the end of their journey, and he knows it. Perhaps he's scared for Lily, or maybe he's just sad because he knows she will be going soon."

"So, do you think he's in on the plan?" Houston asked.

"I'm really not sure. The boy knowing that Lily is leaving just seems like a logical stressor. I suppose it might be something else."

Houston refocused on the road when we reached a narrow section that seemed to hug the side of a cliff with a sharp drop off. The section was short but intense since one wrong move could mean death for all of us. Once he cleared that section of the road, he asked me if I had thought about the best place to pull off the road and continue our journey on the snowmobiles. I wanted to look at the maps again, so I took off my seat belt, turned around, and leaned over the seat into the back. Of course, I realized after it was much too late that in doing what I had, I'd probably stuck my backside almost directly in Houston's face. At least I had lots of clothes on, so nothing would have been too defined.

Once I had the map, I put my seatbelt back on and unrolled it on my lap. I looked at the map, and then I looked around at the landscape. "There's a seasonal road that veers from this road and accesses the cabins in the summer. It won't have been plowed, but I'm still hoping there will be some sort of indication as to where it is. Maybe this road will widen for the turn or something. It should be directly across from the cross on the hill, which we are close to lining up with, so I guess we should look for a widening of the road.

Since we won't be able to access the road, we don't need to line ourselves up exactly, but it will provide a clear trail to follow if we can find it."

"How far will we need to travel once we switch over to the snowmobiles?"

"Not far. Maybe five miles or so. If possible, we'll want to stay out of the trees. If we lose sight of the mountain, it will be hard to keep our bearings, although my watch does have a compass, and I'm pretty good at finding my way using it alone."

"Okay. Let's try to find the road if we can. If we have to venture into the trees, we'll be sure we get a solid compass reading first."

Luckily, we did find the road that veered off toward the cabins, and the road did widen, providing a place to park. Not only did we find that the road was both cleared of trees and wide, but there were other snowmobile tracks that had packed the snow down to a degree. Due to their search-and-rescue training, both dogs knew how to ride on snowmobiles, but since they hadn't gotten much exercise the past couple of days, we decided to allow them to run along next to us for the first mile or until they got tired.

The snowmobile tracks that had previously been cut seemed to go in both directions, indicating that someone may have accessed the cabin and then returned to the road. In fact, I realized as I slowed and looked even closer that it looked like the road had been accessed by more than one machine. Either that or someone had gone back and forth more than once.

After a mile or so, we called the dogs up onto the machines. After a couple more miles, we stopped when we came to the spot where the tracks veered off in two different directions. I cut my motor and waited for Houston to pull up beside me and cut his. We both pulled off our helmets as the dogs jumped down and ran around a bit while we decided what to do.

"Which set of tracks do we follow?" Houston asked.

"I'm not sure," I answered. "The cabins should be straight ahead, but the tracks that veer off into the trees seem more recent."

Houston hesitated before he spoke. "I suppose the recent set of tracks could have been made by someone out for a reason having nothing to do with the kidnapped girls."

"That's true."

"We know the girls are in a cabin, and we didn't see any cabins on the map this close to the main road, which makes me think we should just continue on the road."

I glanced at both the tracks on the road and the tracks that headed into the trees. "The tracks that head into the trees travel in both directions, so someone has gone toward something in the forested area and come out. It might be hunters, but we are pretty far out. Let's let the dogs choose."

"Okay. I suppose that's as good a plan as any."

Once the dogs had been given their instructions, they set off into the trees, so Houston and I followed them. When the tree cover became dense, we were forced to travel single file. I went first, following the dogs, and Houston fell in behind me. We didn't have to travel far before a cabin that hadn't been on the map we'd been looking at came into sight. If anyone was there, they should have heard us, so I didn't think it was a good sign that no one came out to see what was going on. We killed the engines and slipped off the machines. Houston pulled his gun, I accessed mine, we instructed the dogs to walk behind us, and then we slowly headed toward the front door.

Houston knocked, instructing me to stand off to the side. When no one answered, he tried the knob. It was locked. There were snowmobile tracks everywhere, so even though all the windows were boarded up, it was obvious someone had been here recently. If the person who was staying in the cabin was simply a hunter who was out and would return, he was going to be angry if we damaged the place, but Houston and I both knew we couldn't leave without looking inside, so he shot out the lock and kicked in the door.

The first thing I noticed was the stench. The second thing I noticed was the old woman who'd been feeding the girls, still sitting in the same chair she'd been sitting in during both my visits yesterday.

"She's dead," I said, taking a few steps into the interior for a better look. "I'd say she's been gone for around twenty-four hours. Both times I made contact yesterday, I could see her sitting exactly like this in this chair." I glanced down the hallway. There was no one else in this part of the cabin, so I assumed that the group fled, but we did need to check. Houston and I headed down the hallway, checking the rooms beyond the doors, but all were empty.

"Do you think he killed her?" I asked after we returned to the front porch to escape the smell of decomposition.

"I don't know for certain, but it didn't look as if she met with violence," Houston said. "She was an old woman. The man with the ski mask has been dragging her around in the cold for at least two weeks. Chances are she fell ill and passed naturally." He pulled the door closed. "When we get back to town, I'll contact local law enforcement. They can send someone out to retrieve the body."

I blew out a breath of frustration. "So what do we do now?"

"I guess we need to regroup. I hate to ask this of you, but it might help us to know where the group went off to if you can connect with the boy again."

"Yeah." I sighed. "I thought of that. Let's head back to the truck, and I'll give it a try."

We called the dogs to ride with us the entire way on the return trip to the truck, making the return trip a bit faster than the trip out to the cabin had been. Once we were settled inside, Houston cranked the heater up, and I closed my eyes and tried to focus. At first, I got nothing. Not an emotion. Not a flash of memory. Nothing. But I kept at it even though my head felt as if it was going to split in two, and I eventually began to pick up on a distinct feeling of fear and uncertainty.

I could still feel Jeremy blocking me. I really needed to work with him. He'd shut me out when I'd envisioned Laura, so I tried to bring Lily to mind. Hopefully, Lily was still alive and still with them. Hopefully, Jeremy still wanted to help her.

"I have something," I whispered, afraid of breaking the link but wanting to let Houston know not to speak to me from that point forward.

I sensed the feeling of fear and latched on. It was difficult to know how to communicate with the boy since he apparently didn't understand words. Usually, I'd simply "say" what I wanted to say to those I connected with, but I had to think in images with Jeremy. I thought about the cabin we'd just left. I thought about the old woman in the chair. I thought about the empty rooms and hoped he was picking up on my fear in relation to those empty rooms.

I pictured Lily. I visualized her being free to run to her mother, whose image I'd never actually seen, so I had to create a woman in my mind that could be Lily's mother. I hoped that Jeremy would pick up on my hope and longing. I hoped he'd start to trust me.

Eventually, I felt the wall he'd erected begin to break down. I could feel both his fear and his longing to help Lily. She was the key, so I really focused in on her. I was eventually able to see Lily sitting by a fire that had been built outdoors. She was sitting on a log that was lying across the top of the snow. I was pretty sure they were out in the forest somewhere in the area, but all I could see was snow and trees, making it impossible to hone in on a location.

I desperately tried to see some sort of landmark, but the tree cover was too dense. Eventually, Jeremy must have realized this, and he must have wanted to help since he fed me a memory. One of his memories.

I watched as a middle-aged man, built like Goliath, came into the cabin. He saw the old woman in the chair and said something to the boy whose memory I was sharing. I, of course, couldn't hear what he'd said since Jeremy couldn't hear what he said, but I got the gist of things as the man went down the hallway and came back with the dark-haired girl. Jeremy must have followed the man outside because his memory showed him following the man. There was another girl, bound and gagged on the back of the snowmobile. Chances are that his reason for being at the cabin was to deliver the third girl while he prepared the others for transport. The middle-aged man said something to Jeremy, which, again, neither of us could hear, but Jeremy seemed to understand that he wanted him to wait with the first girl while he moved the other two to another location. He seemed to know that the man intended to come back for him and the first girl, who we now knew was named Lily.

After the middle-aged man left with the girl with the dark hair and the new girl, Jeremy decided to take Lily. He tossed her a bunch of clothes, and she seemed to know to bundle up. The boy took her hand and then began dragging her away from the cabin. I supposed she may have been exhausted and lagging behind because, after a bit, he picked her up. Jeremy continued for quite a while before he finally stopped and made a fire.

"He's on foot," I said, which unfortunately broke the connection. That was okay since I knew what to do. "We need to go back," I said, pulling on my outerwear. "Jeremy has Lily in the forest. They were on foot. The dogs can find them. I have a feeling if we don't find them, neither of them will make it through the night."

We loaded the dogs onto the snowmobiles and then headed back to the cabin as fast as we could safely travel. Once we arrived at the cabin, I grabbed one of the blankets that the girls had been sleeping on since the blanket would provide the girls' scent to the dogs. I knew the middle-aged man would eventually come back to the cabin for Jeremy and Lily. At least I hoped he would. Maybe we could catch him if he did. Of course, he may have already returned and found the cabin empty and then left again to return to wherever the two girls he still had and must have locked up were.

I really wanted to find the kidnapper and the two girls he still had, but at this moment, the most important thing was to locate Jeremy and Lily before they froze to death.

I let the dogs sniff the blanket, telling them repeatedly, "This is Lily; find Lily." Once the dogs understood what I was asking and were on the move, we followed them.

Luckily, the dogs managed to pick the trail up right away. The snow was deep, but since the snow hadn't fallen recently, it had settled and iced up, making it easier for the dogs to walk on. Houston and I followed the dogs with the snowmobiles as best we could. It seemed like the dogs wound themselves in and out of the trees in a random pattern that didn't make a lot of sense, but in the vision Jeremy had shared, he and Lily had been running away from the cabin and the eventual return of the man with the ski mask, so I supposed putting distance between themselves and the cabin, was more important than arriving at any sort of preconceived destination.

We'd actually made it pretty far before I noticed haze from the fire they'd built that currently marred the sky. Right after I noticed the smoke, the dogs barked and took off running. I heard someone who I assumed was Lily scream for help. Within minutes, we had both Jeremy and Lily on the snowmobiles, with the dogs following behind as we made our way back to the truck.

Chapter 12

It took a bit longer to make it back to the truck with the dogs on foot, but they were young, energetic dogs who actually managed to keep up quite nicely. When we arrived at the truck, Houston loaded up the snowmobiles while I started the truck and got the heater going. Jeremy opted to sit in the back, and both dogs jumped in beside him, so I wrapped Lily up in a blanket and settled her onto the front passenger seat. Once the snowmobiles were loaded, I climbed in through the driver's side door and sat in the middle, and then Houston climbed in beside me. Once the radio in Houston's truck was in range, he called to the town where we'd been staying and let local law enforcement know about the body we'd discovered, who we had with us, and that we were on our way in. We didn't have cell reception and wouldn't until we got closer to town, so the police officer Houston spoke to assured him that he'd call Lily's parents.

During the drive back, Jeremy was predictably quiet, although I could tell that he was relieved that Lily was safe. He was a huge boy who, while only fifteen, was as tall and stocky as any fully-grown man I'd ever met. While Jeremy sat silently during the long drive back to the inn, Lily was a regular chatterbox once she'd warmed up. I had to admit that the girl was resilient. She'd just been through a terrifying ordeal, but once she got started sharing her story, her overall tone and approach seemed almost animated.

She started her story at the beginning. She told us about being approached from behind and never seeing who grabbed her before waking up in a cold and drafty cabin. She talked about how terrified she'd been during those first days. She thought for sure the man who'd taken her was going to kill her or worse, but after a couple of days with no sight of him, she began to relax. After several days, she wasn't sure how many, Bella showed up, and they moved to a different cabin. She shared that she tried to make things easier on Bella by assuring her that no one seemed interested in hurting them. At least not immediately. She'd overheard a man talking outside the room she'd been locked in the first time they'd stopped. She didn't hear everything he said, and she didn't know who he was talking to, but he mentioned something about needing three. Lily assumed that the man meant three girls, and she decided then and there that until they had three, they were probably safe, so she decided to center her attention on finding a way to escape. The old woman who delivered the food never hurt her, nor did she ever talk to her, but the boy who followed along on her visits seemed interested, so she decided to try to connect with him. When she was afforded the chance to do so, she'd make eye contact and then smile at him. He never said a word to her, but he eventually began to seek her out, and over time, he even began to smile back.

She asked about Bella, and I told her that she was safe at home with her parents. Then I asked her to tell me about what had happened in the last twenty-four hours that led to her being out in the woods with Jeremy. When I said Jeremy's name, she turned her head, looked behind her, and smiled at him. He shyly smiled back.

"The old woman who'd been feeding us made me leave with her and Jeremy, but we left Bella behind. I guess there wasn't room for everyone." She paused. "I'm glad you found her. When she wasn't with us, I was afraid that they'd killed her."

I took Lily's hand and gave it a squeeze in an offer of support and encouragement to continue.

"After we met up with the man with the ski mask, he took Emily and then moved us to the cabin where you found us. I knew he needed three, and at that point, he only had two, so I wasn't surprised when he turned up with another girl today. I expected that they'd toss her in with Emily and me, or maybe they'd take all three of us to another location, but instead, a man, who I was sure was the man in the ski mask, although today he didn't have a ski mask, came in and grabbed Emily and me. At first, he was going to try to take all of us at the same time, but I guess he realized that wouldn't work, so he told Jeremy to watch me. He tied my hands and shoved me toward the cabin before he put the girl he'd brought with him, who was still tied up, and Emily on his snowmobile and left. Jeremy was supposed to take me back inside, and he did at first, but when I saw that the old woman who'd been bringing the food was dead, I totally freaked out. Jeremy wanted to calm me down, but I wanted to leave. I think he knew that since he had me bundle up and took my hand. He led me out into the forest. I was scared because we were heading out on foot, but the alternative, which was to wait for the man to come back, seemed worse, so I tried to keep up with him. Eventually, he picked me up and carried me. After we were far enough away from the cabin, he stopped and built a fire. It was then that you found us."

"Do you know if the man with the ski mask ever came back for you?" I asked.

She shook her head. "I don't know. We left right after he did."

"Did anyone mention the name of the third girl he brought with him today?"

"No. I don't think so."

"Do you know where the man who took you was heading?" Houston jumped in.

She shook her head. "No. I don't know. He wasn't around much. He would only show up to drop someone off or move us, and even then, he rarely spoke to us."

"Did the old woman with the food ever mention anything that might provide a clue about where they were heading?" I asked.

She shook her head. "No. She never spoke to us the entire time we were being held."

Lily continued to chat with us, answering all the questions she could as we continued to head south. By the time we'd arrived in town and had taken Lily and Jeremy to the inn where the local police were supposed to meet us, it had been determined that the girl on the snowmobile who Lily had seen that morning was probably Irene Bowman. Irene had been missing from town since the previous afternoon.

"If the man with the ski mask has Emily and Irene, then he has two," Lily said. "I doubt he'll wait to take a third girl." Her voice rose just a bit. "You need to find him. You need to find him *before* he gets three."

"We will," I promised her, even though I really had nothing to base that promise on.

I had to admit that Lily was a real trooper. When a man who introduced himself as Officer Preston sat her down and began asking her questions, she jumped right in with articulate answers that far exceeded the sort of response one might expect from a girl her age. Not only was the girl obviously bright, but Lily had spunk and confidence not always found in someone so young. I had the feeling that whatever she chose to do in life, she was going to be hugely successful.

Once the police had interviewed Lily, they turned their attention to Jeremy, but he, of course, couldn't speak. I could see that Officer Preston was becoming frustrated with the mute teenager, so I asked everyone to leave Jeremy and me alone for a few minutes. I figured that if I could connect with him, we could communicate that way. He didn't hesitate to let me in this time. I imagined the man who fit the description Lily had given us. I shrugged and then pointed to a map. Jeremy looked at the map and then pointed to a small town on the sea named Barron.

"The man is taking the girls to Barron?" I asked, even though I knew the boy couldn't hear me. He must have "heard" my intent because he pointed at the map again. He closed his eyes and imagined the man Lily had described as well as two other men. He imagined them taking the girls and putting them on a small cargo plane.

"The man with the ski mask is taking the girls to Barron," I said again, only this time it was a statement and not a question.

After I shared my belief with Houston that the man with the girls was taking them to meet up with someone who would transport them wherever they were being sent, he called and gave the Barron PD a heads up. Then he got on the phone and began looking for a private plane to take us north.

Lily's parents were making plans to come for her, but we really weren't sure what to do with Jeremy. As far as I was concerned, he was a victim rather than an accomplice, but because he'd often been alone with the girls and could probably have found a way to act sooner, things were murky. Still, Houston agreed that he didn't want to leave him in jail with local law enforcement or return him to his abusive father, so in the end, I called Jake and Dani. Dani agreed to fly Jake and Wyatt to the town where we were staying, and Jake would take over custody of Jeremy until we got back, and Wyatt would drive Houston's truck back to Rescue.

When Dani and Jake showed up, Jeremy seemed terrified, but Lily helped me convince him that going with them was the best thing for him, so he willingly went along when directed to do so. He seemed a bit less terrified when it was decided that Lily would go with Jake and Dani in the chopper and meet up with her parents in Rescue.

"I found a plane," Houston said after we'd seen Dani off with Jake, Jeremy, and Lily. Wyatt and the dogs were going to stay in one of the rooms we'd already paid for and make the drive back to Rescue tomorrow.

"Can he take us tonight?"

"He can. I told him we'd meet him at the airfield in an hour."

"Do you really think we can find this guy and the girls he has with him before it's too late?"

"I'm going to try. I have my men meeting with Jake and Jeremy when they get back. I'm hoping that if Jeremy looks through a book of mug shots, he'll recognize someone. Or maybe they can get him to draw the man he was with or the man he was planning to meet. Barron is a small town. If he's there, we'll find him."

I thought about the little town, which was shrouded in twenty-four hours of darkness during this time of the year. I realized that finding a specific man I'd never seen before in a town without daylight was not going to be an easy thing to do. Still, he was traveling with at least two girls. Three if he'd snagged one to replace Lily. How many middle-aged men could there be in this tiny northern town with two or three preteen girls tagging along with him?

Chapter 13

Now that Lily was safe, Jeremy was no longer trying to pull me in or keep me away. This led to an almost immediate lessening of my headache, although I was sure it would be days before it dissipated completely. I had an image of the man who'd kidnapped the girls in my mind that Jeremy had shared with me. Assuming it was an accurate image, I hoped that knowing what the man we were searching for looked like would help us find him if he was, as we had hoped, headed toward Barron.

Once Houston and I boarded the plane for our trip north, I promptly put my head on his shoulder and fell asleep. By the time we reached Barron, I felt marginally better. I was glad the pounding in my head had lessened to the point where I could actually function since I had a feeling the next twenty-four hours were going to be long ones.

A police officer named Dru Belmont picked us up at the airstrip. He took us back to his office in Barron, where Houston filled him in on everything that had occurred to this point, and I searched the computer for images of men known to work in human trafficking. The problem was that there were too many to consider. I needed to pare things down a bit. Houston and Dru were busy talking in Dru's office, so I used my cell phone to call my good friend, fellow search-and-rescue volunteer, computer geek, and all-around nice guy, Landon Stanford.

"Harmony. I'm glad you called. I've been worried about you."

"I'm fine," I rotely responded.

"Still having the headaches?"

"A bit, but they're better. I guess you heard that we rescued the boy I've been connecting with and the first girl who was taken."

"Yeah. I talked to Jake. I'm really glad these kids are safe, but it sounds like this madman has two others."

"He does," I confirmed. "Two girls, both twelve. One is named Emily Deerchild, and the other is Irene Bowman. He may have a third girl by this point, although I don't know that with any certainty. I suppose if he's headed toward Barron, where I assume he's going to hand off the girls, he must be running out of time."

"Yeah. It would seem he might be. How can I help?"

"I'm sitting here in the office of the man who seems to be law enforcement in Barron, looking at images on his computer. I was able to get a look at the kidnapper through Jeremy's memories, so they have me looking at mugshots of men who are known to work in human trafficking, but there are so many. I need to organize them. Pare them down. Houston is busy, so I'm hoping you can help me."

"I can. If you can get permission for me to link into the database you're searching, I can take a look."

"Okay. Hang on."

I got up and crossed the room. I knocked on the door of the interrogation room where Houston was sitting talking to Dru. I explained who I had on the phone and what I wanted him to do, and Dru agreed to give him access. Once Landon had access, he took control of the search. He'd send photos to me, which I commented on, then he made modifications and searched again. By the time Dru and Houston emerged from the room where they'd been chatting, we had a name.

"Carl Decker," I said.

Both men just looked at me.

"Carl Decker is the name of the man with the girls." I turned the computer screen toward the men. "Landon helped me find him. He isn't in the database of known human traffickers, but he does have a record."

Houston pulled the computer closer and took a look. "Armed robbery, domestic violence, assault, and manslaughter." He looked up at me. "Are you sure this is him?"

"This is the man who was in Jeremy's head."

Houston turned and looked at Dru. "Do you recognize this man?"

"No. But now that we have a name and image, we can ask around." He glanced at the clock. "Things will be in full swing at Hades. I guess we can start there."

"Hades?" I asked.

"Local bar."

I supposed as names of bars might go, Hades was original, but, in my opinion, not nearly as charming as Neverland.

"Give me a minute to make a call, and I'll go with you," Dru said. "The locals in these parts don't take kindly to strangers and probably won't tell you a thing even if they have something to tell."

Houston thanked him, and the two of us took seats at the table where I'd been working while we waited.

"I heard from Jordan," he said. Jordan was Jake's girlfriend and a doctor. "She's waiting for the full autopsy report, but she said it appears that the old woman we found in the cabin died of natural causes."

"I didn't know they'd already retrieved the body."

He nodded. "They used snowmobiles with a rescue sled to go in for her. Jordan called and spoke to the only doctor in Huntsville, and he did a preliminary exam. He's having the body transported to Fairbanks for autopsy, but the initial exam didn't reveal any signs of foul play. It appears she just sat down in the chair where we found her and passed peacefully."

Well, I supposed that was something. I still didn't have a feel for the old woman's role in the whole thing. Was she willingly with the kidnapper, or was she a victim?

"Do you have an identity?" I asked.

He nodded. "Daisy Dunsmore. She used to run a foster home in a small town in Western Canada, but she sold her property and moved away a decade ago. I haven't found a record of her whereabouts since then. I suppose she might have left with Carl willingly, but I also suppose he might have kidnapped her at some point."

"I wonder how they knew each other."

Houston shrugged. "I'm not sure. I suppose if we catch up with him, we can ask him, but if I had to guess, I suspect that Carl was a foster child and Daisy was the woman who cared for him."

"That does make sense. I wonder why Lily called her Fran?"

He shrugged. "I suppose Fran might just be a name Lily made up if she didn't know the old woman's actual name. It doesn't sound like she talked to the girls."

"That's true. Maybe giving her a name made it easier to communicate with her even if the name Lily gave her wasn't her real name."

Houston and I both looked up as Dru came back into the room. "Okay," he said. "I'm all set. Let's head over to Hades and see if anyone has seen your guy."

As it turned out, several men had seen him, just not recently. One of the bar's patrons claimed a man who looked an awful lot like the photo was seen in town last winter, and another patron claimed to have seen him the year before that. We'd suspected this wasn't our kidnapper's first time doing what he was doing, and the statements of the men we spoke to seemed to confirm that.

Houston and I decided to hang out in the bar for a while and talk to other men and women as they came in. Dru got a call and went outside to take it. When he came back inside, he had a frown on his face.

"What happened?" I asked.

"Sarah Farmington, a local girl, went missing."

I put a hand to my mouth. "Oh, no," I gasped. "The third girl."

"It looks like that might be the case," Dru responded. "I'm heading over to talk to her parents."

"If he has three, he might be planning to meet his contact as soon as this evening," I said. "We need to find them, and we need to find them fast."

"Any idea where the meeting might be taking place?" Houston asked.

"We assume the person who our kidnapper is handing these girls off to is a pilot," I added.

"I'm afraid that if the man has a bush plane, there are a lot of places he could land in this area," Dru answered.

"He needs to keep the girls somewhere until the meeting, and it will be close," I said. "He's missing both his helpers, so he's on his own. He won't go to a motel since it would be hard to hide three girls in a place like that. What about a cabin? A seasonal cabin would work best. Something out of the way, but not too far away. Something with boarded up windows and little chance that anyone will stop by."

"There are some seasonal cabins near the sea just west of here." Dru looked undecided. "I really should go and talk to Sarah's parents."

"We can go and check out the cabins if you have a vehicle you can lend us," I offered. "We'll call you if we find anything."

"I have a truck at my house with a snowmobile all loaded in the bed. It never hurts to be prepared. We'll stop by and get it. I'll head over to talk to the parents, and you can see if there is any sign of life in the cabins."

"Sounds like a plan," I said.

"I'll send Mucker with you."

"Mucker?" I asked.

"Mucker's my dog. He's search-and-rescue trained. If this man is holding the girls in one of those cabins, he'll find 'em. If you do find this guy, hang back and wait for me. We don't know if he's armed, but if he is, I don't want anyone getting hurt."

Houston and I both had guns and knew how to use them. I wasn't worried about heading out to the cabin on our own, but I was curious why there weren't men in town who'd been designated to help when needed. Sure, the town was tiny, and I had a feeling it was the sort of place where folks mostly did what they wanted, laws be damned, but I really couldn't see how one man could run things on his own. Of course, Houston and I had only been sent out to the cabins to take a look and see if we could find the girls. I supposed that if a hostage situation occurred, Dru would have men he could call in.

"Do you really think this guy is holed up in one of these cabins?" I asked Houston as we drove west with Dru's dog, Mucker, in the back seat. The dog seemed thrilled to be along for the ride, and I had to admit that his happy face was making me miss my happy dogs.

"Honestly, not really. Given what we already know about this guy, I think the cabins are too obvious. Unless he's totally clueless, I think he would realize that these sorts of cabins are exactly where we'd be looking for him."

"Yeah, it seems like a longshot to me as well, but so far, no one has come up with a better idea. I guess it doesn't hurt to take a look." I glanced up into the dark sky. "It would help if we had some daylight, but I guess that isn't going to happen."

"Not for another couple of weeks."

"You'd think that after living in Rescue my entire life, I'd be used to the long dark days, but at least we get a few hours of sunlight even in the middle of winter. I'm not sure how it would be to have more than two months of darkness to deal with every year."

"I guess you get used to it."

"I guess." I glanced out at the barren landscape. It really was beautiful in its own way.

"In a way, it's too bad we rescued Jeremy," Houston said. "Not that I'm not delighted to help the boy find his way out of an impossible situation, and not that I'm not thrilled that Lily was rescued, but he was your link to the man with the girls. It'll be a lot harder to track him down without a bird's-eye view."

Mucker stuck his head over the back of the seat, and I gave him a scratch under the chin. "Yeah. That thought has occurred to me as well." I turned my head to look out the window again. "I guess I can try to connect with one of the girls. I have names and faces now, so that will help. Even if I can find them, they'll need to let me in, and there's no guarantee of that happening."

Houston's lips tightened. "Maybe you should try to connect with them. I know that doing so causes you pain, and I really hate to ask, but I have a feeling that we're running out of time. Once this man hands the girls off to whoever he's here to hand them off to, assuming we're correct in our theory and that's what's going on, it's unlikely we'll ever find them."

"Yeah. I thought of that too." I took a deep breath and closed my eyes. "I may speak to you, but try not to speak to me and don't ask me any questions unless you absolutely have to."

"Okay," Houston nodded.

I leaned my head back against the headrest and closed my eyes. I focused on the steady hum of the engine as I tried to create an image of Emily in my mind. Of the girls who were currently being held, she'd been with the kidnapper the longest. Chances were that she was the calmest at this point and would therefore be the easiest to connect with.

I willed an image of twelve-year-old Emily Deerchild into my mind. Brown hair, blue eyes, slight build, and engaging smile. At least she'd been smiling in the photo her parents had submitted when they'd reported her missing. I let the image develop and willed specific details to come to mind. The long ponytail, hanging off to the side, the small dimple on the left side of her mouth, the scar across her forehead that had probably been earned fairly early in life.

Unlike Jeremy, Emily had words, so I used words to call to her.

"Emily," I thought in my mind as I focused on her image. "My name is Harmony. I want to help you. Can you hear me?"

I didn't hear anything at first, so I tried again.

"I'm with the police. We are coming to get you, but I need your help."

"Who are you? Why can I hear you, but I can't see you?"

I smiled when I realized that I'd made it through. "My name is Harmony. I'm sort of a psychic. I can't tell the future or anything like that, but I can get into people's minds. I want to help you, but you need to let me in."

I could feel her resisting.

"Please," I deepened my focus. "We found Lily. She's safe with her parents. She told us about you, and we want to help. We will help, but you need to let me in."

"How do I let you in?"

"Just relax. I'm going to try to see what you see through your eyes. I'm going to talk to you in your mind, and I'll need you to answer me back by thinking of your answer. Are you alone?"

"No. There are three of us."

"Is the man who took you there?"

"No. The man locked us in a room and left. He was on the phone before he left. He was talking to someone about meeting a plane. I think he went to talk to the man he'd been talking to on the phone."

"Okay. That's great. You're doing great. Now, just relax and let me see what you see."

It took a few minutes, but when I was finally able to see what Emily was looking at, it really didn't help.

I could sense a small room with no windows, but it was almost totally dark.

"Can you see outside?" I asked. "Are there any windows in the room?"

"No. I think we're in a storage closet of some sort. There's nothing other than walls and doors. Can I tell the others you're here in my head?"

"Not yet. Let's see what we can figure out first. Just continue talking to me in your mind. Jeremy, the boy who was in the cabin with you, told me that the man who kidnapped you took you and Irene away on his snowmobile."

"Yes. That's right. The boy could talk?"

"No. I spoke to Jeremy in his mind the way I'm speaking to you. I'll fill you in later. What happened after he took you away on his snowmobile?"

"He brought us to a plane. He tied us up, put us in the plane, and then he left again. A long time later, he came back alone. He was really mad. I thought he might kill us out of anger, but he didn't."

"Do you know why he was mad?"

"He was mad 'cause the others were gone."

"Okay. What happened after the man came back alone?"

"He took off and brought us here."

"So he flew the plane himself?"

"Yes. He flew it himself."

Okay, that was helpful. "And after you landed? What happened then?"

"He blindfolded Irene and me and brought us to this closet. Then he left. A little while ago, he brought another girl. He threw her inside with us and left again."

"Did you travel far to get to the closet after you left the plane?"

"No. Maybe ten minutes."

Ten minutes. The girls were definitely not all the way out here in these cabins unless the man landed the plane somewhere other than the main airstrip, which was likely now that I thought about it. "I know you can't see anything, but can you hear anything?"

"Music."

I was so shocked by the answer that I almost lost the connection. "Music? What sort of music?"

"I don't know. It's not a song I recognize. It sounds far away, but it's so loud I can hear it."

"I'm going to break the connection for a minute. I need to talk to someone. I'm going to come back in a few minutes, so try to keep your mind open and wait for me."

"Where are you going? Are you still going to help us?"

"I am. I need to tell the police officer I'm with where to find you. Just wait quietly for a couple minutes, and I'll be back."

"Okay, but hurry."

I opened my eyes and looked at Houston. "The girls aren't all the way out here in one of these cabins. They're closer to town. In a closet of some sort. Emily said she could hear music in the distance."

"The bar."

"That would be my guess. We need to go back."

"I'll call Dru."

"Wait," I said. "I'm not sure we should call Dru."

"Why not?"

"I'm not sure, but something feels off to me. Let's just go back and see what we can find. We can call Dru after we check things out."

Houston turned the truck around and headed back. When we arrived at the bar, we parked out in front and just sat for a minute. If the girls were being held inside the bar, maybe the bar owner was in on things. The entire place was packed with rugged outdoorsmen whose loyalty would be to one of their own, so it didn't seem smart to just push our way in and start accusing those who are inside of harboring a kidnapper.

"I'm going to try to connect again. Give me a minute," I said.

This time, Emily was waiting for me and let me in right away.

"I was scared you wouldn't come back."

"I'm here. Can you still hear the music?"

"Yes."

"Focus on it. I want to hear it."

It took a minute, but a sound eventually came through. I immediately knew that the music she heard was different than the music coming from the bar. I wondered if there was another bar in Barron. Probably. The entire town was only a few blocks in all directions, so I instructed Houston to drive around. Eventually, we found a bar playing the same music Emily could hear.

"I found you," I said in my thoughts. "Or at least I found the music. I want you to snuggle up with the others and keep quiet. I'm going to look for you. If I need you to do something, I'll come back and tell you."

"Okay, but hurry. I'm so, so scared."

I bet she was. I couldn't imagine having to endure something like the ordeal she'd been through, especially for a twelve-year-old.

"Should we go in and look around?" Houston said.

"No. The music is muted, and the bar is small. I don't think the girls are in the bar." I looked around at the building near the bar. "There," I pointed at a warehouse-type building. "Let's look there."

We got out of the truck, taking Mucker with us. We hurried through the night to the warehouse, which looked to be abandoned. When we found a broken window in the back, Houston climbed through and opened a side door for Mucker and me. Mucker immediately took off into the darkness. By the time

Houston and I caught up with him, we could hear the girls banging on the door. Houston called for them to stand back, and then he kicked it in. All three girls looked terrified, but when Emily saw me, she left the others to throw herself into my arms.

Chapter 14

After we'd rescued the girls, we repeatedly tried to call Dru, but he wasn't picking up. We realized the kidnapper would be back for the girls and that our best bet at capturing him was to simply wait for him to arrive, so Houston stayed at the warehouse while I took the girls with me to Sarah's home. When I arrived at Sarah's home, I hoped Dru would still be there, but Sarah's parents informed me that he'd never shown up for the interview. I'd had a bad feeling about things for a while, and my inability to locate the guy was only making that feeling worse.

Houston called to let me know that he'd called and spoken to Preston in Huntsville while he'd waited at the warehouse. He wanted to let him know that we had Irene. Preston was thrilled we'd found the girl and arranged for a pilot he knew to bring her parents to Barron to escort her home. Emily was taken closer to Rescue, so Houston and I figured we'd just take her home with us. He'd called her parents to let them know she was safe and would be returned shortly.

Of course, before we did that, we really needed to find both Dru and the kidnapper.

"Hey, Houston, any updates?" I asked after I dropped the girls off, and Mucker and I returned to the truck Dru had lent us.

"No. I'm still sitting here waiting. How did things go on your end?"

"Fantastic, as you can imagine. Sarah's parents were so relieved and happy to see her. It really did my heart good." I supposed it was these happy reunions that I found to be the most gratifying thing about search-and-rescue.

"And the other girls?"

"Sarah's parents were happy to allow Emily and Irene to stay with them until someone came for them, so I think we're all set there."

"Do Sarah's parents seem capable of protecting the girls in the unlikely event that the kidnapper tries to get his property back?" Houston asked.

"They do. Sarah's father is an ex-marine and volunteer firefighter. He knows his way around a gun and seems capable of keeping the girls safe. Given everything that's going on, leaving all the girls with him seemed the best option."

"Yeah, it sounds like you made a wise decision. Are you heading back here?"

"Not yet. I'm going to stop by the police station and take a look around, and if Dru isn't there, then I'm going to take a look at his home. If I can't figure out where he went, I'll come to you. I'll call you either way."

"I don't like you snooping around on your own. The man who took these girls is still out there, and you know he's going to be mad once he figures out that all his hard work the past few weeks has been for naught."

"I'm totally capable of looking out for myself." I looked down at the large dog. "Besides, I have Mucker to keep me safe. You're the one who needs to be careful. As you just pointed out, when the kidnapper gets back and finds the storage room empty, he's going to be mad."

"Let's just hope he does come back. If he somehow found out that we have the girls, I will have been sitting here in the dark and cold for nothing." He took a breath. "I'll call Emily's parents and let them know she's been found safe and that we'll bring her home once we're done here. I called Preston, but I'm not sure he has their contact information."

"I'm sure Preston can get it, but I'm sure Emily's parents would appreciate a call from you." I glanced out the window at the endless night. "I should get going. I'll call you back in a bit."

After I hung up with Houston, I headed toward the police station. It was dark and locked up tight. I considered trying to break in but decided against it at this point. Then I headed over to Dru's home. It was dark too. I didn't know the area and realized that I'd need help tracking the man down. I thought about the men at Hades. Dru seemed to know everyone well. I had no way of knowing if the local police officer was dead or alive at this point, but I did know I needed to find him fast, so I headed back in the direction of the bar. I took Mucker inside with me since I figured I'd need to prove I had Dru's best interests at heart when I spoke to the men. As soon as I opened the front door to the establishment, Mucker trotted in and headed directly over to a man with a thick black beard. It seemed Mucker had chosen. This man, I decided, was the one I'd confide in.

"Hey, Mucker." The man smiled. He glanced at me. "Is Dru with you?"

"Actually, no. My name is Harmony Carson. Do you think we can chat for a few minutes?" I looked around the room. "In private."

The man looked undecided, but then he glanced down at Mucker and shrugged. "Sure. I guess. My name is Ed. Ed Valdez." He stood up and took my arm. "There's a room in the back. It's usually empty at this time of the day."

I followed the man down a short hallway to an empty room. He flipped the light on and motioned for me to have a seat. Once seated, I launched into my story, keeping it brief but being sure to cover all the important details. The longer I spoke, the deeper the man's frown line creased into his forehead.

After a minute, he took out his cell phone. He tried a number and then hung up. "You said that you followed Dru to his home, where he gave you his truck to drive and hooked you up with Mucker."

"Yes. We were going to head to the seasonal cabins on the sea when I had an intuition to check the warehouse where we ended up finding the girls."

"Intuition?"

"It's a long story, and I don't know that we have a lot of time. My friend, Police Chief Hank Houston, of Rescue, Alaska's police department, is waiting at the warehouse, hoping the kidnapper will return for the girls. I was supposed to take Sarah home and find somewhere safe for the other two girls to wait, but when I arrived and spoke to Sarah's parents, they said that Dru had never shown up for the interview. He specifically said that was where he was going after he saw Houston and me off. I'm worried that something has happened to him and decided it might be a good idea to bring someone local in on the situation. I just met the man tonight, and we only spoke for a few minutes. I figured I needed to bring someone in who knew Dru better than I do and would be better able to anticipate his actions to give me a place to begin the search."

"And why did you choose me?"

"I didn't. Mucker did. I just opened the door to the bar where Dru had introduced us around earlier, and Mucker came directly to you, so I figured if he trusted you, I trusted you."

That had the man smiling. "Okay," he said. "You head back to your friend and wait for the kidnapper. I'll round up some men and look for Dru. Give me your cell phone number, and I'll give you mine. That way, we can stay in touch."

I did as the man asked.

"If the kidnapper turns up, let me know," he said. "If I find Dru, I'll let you know."

"Okay, great. Hopefully, by the end of this long night of endless night, all the girls will be safely returned to their homes, Dru will have been found safe, and the kidnapper will be behind bars."

Mucker followed Ed when he left, so I headed back to the warehouse on my own. I couldn't get Houston's comment about wasting our time out of my mind and really hoped that wouldn't end up being the case. I did feel good about bringing Ed in on things. I could tell this was the type of town where folks were self-sufficient and took care of their own. Ed struck me as the sort of man who would not only know what to do but whose help would be invaluable in this sort of situation.

When I arrived back at the warehouse, I found Houston sitting behind an old generator. I doubted it was operable since it looked to be rusted and worn, but it was a large unit, which had me wondering what sort of operation this large metal building had been built to house in the first place.

"Any activity?" I asked as I sat down next to Houston.

"Not a thing." I could hear the tone of frustration in his voice.

"The only people who know we found the girls beside you and me are Sarah's parents, Preston from the Huntsville PD, Irene's parents, Emily's parents, and Ed Valdez. It's unlikely that any of the previously mentioned individuals gave our kidnapper a heads up that the girls had been rescued."

"Jeremy knows."

"Jeremy doesn't speak," I reminded him. "Besides, my gut tells me that he isn't one of the bad guys in this scenario."

"Yeah." Houston sighed. "I have the same gut feeling."

"The likelihood that Carl Decker is still operating under the assumption that things are going as planned is high in my mind. If he believes the girls are still here in this warehouse, he'll come back for them."

Houston took my hand in his and gave it a squeeze. "I know you're right. It's just that this waiting is making me nuts."

"I know. Waiting is hard."

He glanced around the room. "Where did you leave the truck?"

"I parked it in the parking area that serves the bar and walked over. When Decker returns, he shouldn't have any reason to believe that anyone is waiting for him. When he comes in, we'll get him, and then this whole long drawn out nightmare can finally come to an end."

"It will be nice to get home. I feel like I could sleep for a week."

"Tell me about it. I think this whole thing has been hard on everyone." I glanced at my cell phone.

"Waiting to hear about Dru?" Houston asked. I imagined he'd noticed my preoccupation with willing my cell phone to ring.

I nodded. "Ed told me he'd stay in touch, but I haven't heard from him since he left with Mucker to look for Dru. I think I'll text him."

"I am concerned that Dru never showed up to talk to Sarah's parents," Houston agreed. "He said that he was heading straight to their place when he left us. He must have had a call or something that sent him off in another direction."

"Yeah. I hope Dru's okay." I continued to stare at my cell phone, willing it to show me a return text from Ed. "It seems like he would have contacted us by now if he simply was called out on another call and had to put off the interview he'd been heading toward."

The face of my cell phone lit up. It was a return text from Ed, letting me know he'd rounded up a team of men he trusted to look for Dru, but that so far, they hadn't found him. He asked how Houston and I were doing, and I texted back to let him know we were still waiting.

"I guess it's a good thing they haven't found him injured or worse," I said, trying for a tone of optimism.

"I'm sure he's fine," Houston said in a tone that made it clear that what he really thought was that Dru was far from fine.

I laid my head on Houston's shoulder. I couldn't believe how tired I was. It was freezing in the warehouse, but I had on enough clothes to make me warm enough that I found myself drifting off to sleep. I really wanted to give in to the urge to take a short nap, but I knew Houston was tired as well, and I also knew we'd never forgive ourselves if we both fell asleep and missed the man we were waiting for.

"I wonder how Wyatt and the dogs are doing," I commented for no other reason than to have something to talk about.

"I'm sure they're doing fine." Houston looked at his watch. "In fact, I'm sure they're still sleeping in one of the large beds we left behind at the inn."

Boy, did I ever wish I was curled up in one of those beds.

"Do you think the kidnapper will even come back tonight?" I asked. "If you really think about it, he might not come back until tomorrow if his contact isn't supposed to arrive until then."

Houston adjusted his position slightly before he answered. "I did consider the fact that we might be sitting here on this cold floor behind this smelly old generator for a day or even longer, depending on Carl

Decker's plans. If Dru wasn't missing, I'd probably talk to him about getting some men to cover shifts, so we didn't have to sit here all night, but with the way things are currently, I guess staying for however long we need to makes sense."

"I guess," I groaned. My backside was already sore from sitting on the cement floor, and I'd only been sitting here for about half an hour. I had a feeling it was going to be a very long night indeed. "I'm going to head back to the truck and see if there's an emergency kit stashed under the seat or behind the backrest. Everyone who lives in Alaska knows to have a kit in their vehicle. Chances are there's a blanket and probably a thermal throw we can snuggle up under."

"I'll go," Houston stood up. "I need to stretch my legs anyway. I doubt this guy will show up while I'm gone, but if he does, keep quiet and just watch what he does. I don't want you confronting him without me."

"Okay. I'll just wait and watch, but hurry. If you're gone too long, I know I'll fall asleep."

Houston got up and headed toward the door while I stayed where I was and waited. Less than three minutes later, I heard someone open the big roll-up door in the front of the building. "That was fast," I said as I noticed Houston walk back into the warehouse empty-handed.

I stood up. "Didn't you find anything?" I asked a second before I noticed the man with a gun walking behind him.

"Whoever that is hiding back there, come on out," the man called.

I hesitated.

"I'm going to count to three. If I don't see you heading in my direction, I'm going to shoot your friend."

I put my hands up and came out of my hiding place. My instinct was to do something proactive, but Carl had a gun, and I noticed that Houston didn't. Carl must have been outside when Houston left to get the emergency kit.

"Drop your weapon," the man said, nodding toward the gun in my hand and pointing his gun directly at Houston's head.

I did as the man instructed.

He told me to walk over to where he was standing with Houston. I did so. He told both Houston and me to walk toward the little storage closet where he'd left the girls. I knew when he reached it and saw that they were gone, he would be furious. He'd probably shoot us just for the heck of it. I knew I should make some sort of move, but the man had his finger on the trigger and the barrel of the gun resting on Houston's back.

"Damn," the man shouted, slamming his gun into Houston's head and then turning to me. I watched Houston slide to the floor. "What'd you do with my girls?"

"I didn't do anything with anyone," I said. "I don't even know what you're talking about." I looked at Houston and then back up toward the man with the gun. "My friend and I gambled away all of our money, so we decided to spend the night in this warehouse. We're meeting up with a friend tomorrow. My friend here went over to the bar to see if there was something in one of the cars he could steal for us to sleep on. The next thing I know, he's walking back in with a gun pointed at his head. What the heck is going on? Why did you hit my friend?" I demanded. "If you want to rob us, rob us, but we don't have any money. This level of violence is totally unnecessary."

Carl looked uncertain. He'd never met either Houston or me, and Houston wasn't wearing his uniform. The story I was telling him could be true.

"If all of that is true, why did you have a gun?"

I raised a brow. "You do realize this is Alaska, don't you? Everyone in these parts has a gun."

He looked toward the broken door to the storage closet. "How long have you been here?"

"Maybe twenty minutes. We were at the bar next door, but they kicked us out, so we decided to just spend the night in here."

"And that door was already broken when you arrived?"

I shrugged. "I guess. Honestly, I didn't notice. Is this your warehouse? Are you mad because we're trespassing?" I looked down at Houston. I was pretty sure he was knocked out and not dead, but there was quite a bit of blood running over his forehead.

"This isn't my warehouse, but I was keeping something here. You didn't see anyone else when you arrived?"

"No." I huffed out a breath. "The place was deserted." I looked down at Houston. "You didn't kill him, did you?"

"I didn't kill him," the man responded. "Yet." He looked around, almost as if he was trying to work out what to do.

"I really should take a look at his head," I said.

The man pointed the gun directly at my head.

"Are you just going to shoot me for no good reason?" I demanded with a lot more bravo than I actually felt.

The man didn't answer.

"Look, I get the fact that someone took your stuff, and you're angry about that, but I really don't know anything about your missing stuff or the girls you're looking for. My friend and I were just looking for a place to sleep, but if this is your warehouse, we can move on."

The man waved his gun, indicating that I should walk toward the room where we'd found the girls. There was another similar room next to the one with the broken door. The man instructed me to open it, which I did. He then instructed me to grab onto Houston's arms and pull him inside. I wasn't thrilled about the fact that the man seemed to plan to leave us here in the warehouse, but it was better than being shot, so I did as he asked. After Houston was inside the room, he told me to take his cell phone out of his pocket and toss it toward him. I did as he asked. He asked me to toss my cell phone toward him and then to go into the room as well. I complied. He then closed the door. I could hear him taking the chain off the door we'd broken down and chaining it to the door of the room where he'd left us. I listened for a minute to see what he'd do. It sounded like he'd left.

My first thought was to make sure that Houston really was alive, so I knelt down and felt for a pulse.

"Houston," I said, gently caressing his cheek. I could feel blood under my hands, but I ignored it. I needed to get him to wake up. "Come on, Houston, I'm not up for being locked in this room without anyone to talk to."

He groaned.

I let out a sigh of relief.

"It's dark, so I can't see your face. Are you in there? Can you hear me?"

"I'm here." He took a long, painful sounding breath. "What happened?"

I gave him the shortened version of the past twenty minutes.

"We need to get out of here," Houston said. "He's going to get away."

"He locked us in a room very similar to the room we found the girls in. I heard him use the chain to secure the door. He took our guns and cell phones."

"Ed knows where we are," Houston said.

"He does, and he'll eventually come for us, but I'm worried about your head injury. We really should get you to the clinic."

"I'm fine."

"You aren't fine. The man hit you hard enough to knock you out for several minutes."

Houston didn't answer.

"How do you feel? Are you dizzy?"

"A little."

I felt my heart racing as I tried to figure out how to get us out of here sooner rather than later. If Dru had been injured or killed, it could be hours before Ed thought to come looking for us.

"I'm going to try to connect with Emily," I said aloud. "I've done it before, and she knows what to expect. If I can connect with her, she can let Sarah's parents know to send help." I looked around but couldn't see a thing. "I'm going to crawl over to the wall and then lean back against it for support. I want you to come with me. You can put your head in my lap if you still feel dizzy."

"I'm okay," Houston said in a tone of voice that sounded more like a groan than anything.

I crawled along the floor until I found the wall. Houston crawled along after me. I sat on the floor and leaned my back against the wall. Houston sat down next to me. I closed my eyes and focused on Emily. It took a few minutes to connect, but I eventually felt her presence.

"Emily, it's Harmony. I need your help."

"Harmony? What's wrong?"

"The kidnapper locked Houston and me in a room right next to the room where you and the other girls were held. Houston is hurt. We need to get out right away. I need you to tell Sarah's dad that he needs to come for us."

"But he'll want to know how I know where you are. What do I tell him?"

"Tell him whatever you need to tell him. Tell him the truth or tell him a lie. Just get him here."

"Okay. I'll do whatever I need to do."

With that, the link was broken. All we could do at this point was to wait.

Chapter 15

Once Sarah's father freed us, Houston was taken, quite against his will, to the local clinic. I was asked to wait in the small seating area, so I decided to check in with Ed, but then I realized I had no cell phone. I guess Carl must have taken ours with him since they were no longer on the floor where I'd tossed them.

"Excuse me," I said to the one and only nurse I'd seen since I'd been here. "I need to make a call. It's sort of important, but my cell phone was misplaced. Do you think I could use your phone for a really quick call?"

She nodded. "Just press nine in order to get a line out."

Wow. Talk about old school. I pressed nine and prayed that Ed would pick up.

"Yeah," he said after only one ring.

"Ed, it's Harmony. I have news, but my cell phone was taken, so I'm borrowing the phone at the clinic. Do you think you can meet me here so I can fill you in?"

"Yeah, I can do that. I'm close by. I'll be there in two minutes."

I thanked the woman, letting her know that if the man I'd come in with asked for me, I'd be right out front. She nodded, barely even looking up from the romance novel she was reading. I supposed on most nights, a clinic such as this one was pretty slow.

As he said he would, Ed pulled into the parking lot in just about two minutes.

"What are you doing here? Were you injured?" he asked, looking me up and down.

"No, but Houston was." I took a few minutes to bring him up to speed.

"So this guy is in the wind?"

"It looks like he is. Any luck finding Dru?"

He blew out a breath. "No. And I've looked everywhere I can think to look."

"When he took us to his home so we could pick up his truck and the dog, he said he was going straight over to Sarah's home to talk to her parents and would meet us after. Something must have happened between him leaving his home and arriving at their home. I suppose he might have been pulled away by another more important call. If he did receive a call, who would he receive it from?"

"I'm not sure. Most folks know to call his cell phone directly."

"Okay," I paused to consider this. "Maybe we can pull Dru's cell phone records. We'll need a computer."

"I'm sure there's a computer in the clinic that we can use. Do you know how to access phone records? I'm afraid that sort of thing is not one of my talents."

"No, but I know someone who can. If you can get me a computer and a phone, I can get the information we need."

Ed came inside with me and told the woman at the desk what we needed. When I'd spoken to her, she'd barely looked up. When Ed came in, she gave him her full attention. Once I had a phone and computer, I called Landon. It was early. Really, really early, so he sounded groggy, but once I explained what was going on and what I needed, he sprang into action. Once he had Dru's cell phone number, it didn't take him long to let me know that no one had called him during the time when he should have been driving toward Sarah Farmington's home.

I looked at Ed. "No go. No one called Dru during the window we're looking at."

"So maybe he was run off the road."

"Did you find his SUV?" I felt frustration well up in my gut as I considered the fact that Dru might very well be dead and Carl might very well get away.

"No. And we did look for it."

I furrowed my brow. "The SUV he was driving was his official police vehicle. Maybe he has a vehicle locator."

Ed just laughed. "I sincerely doubt that sort of thing is in the budget."

"How about his cell phone?" Landon, who was still waiting on the line, asked.

"Of course," I responded. "Can you locate it?"

"I can. Give me a minute."

While I was waiting for Landon to come back on the line, Houston walked into the room where Ed and I were using the phone and computer. I introduced the two men. After introductions were complete, Houston informed me that he was good to go, although he did have a slight concussion and would need to watch for symptoms. After a few minutes, Landon came back on the line and provided me with a set of coordinates.

"Do you have a map?" I asked Ed. "One with longitude and latitude?"

"In my truck. Why?"

"Landon found Dru's cell phone, but he said it appears to be out in the middle of nowhere. I figure we can use the coordinates to find the exact location of the cell phone. Hopefully, once we find that, we'll find Dru."

"Hang on, and I'll get it."

I told Landon I'd call him back as Ed headed out the door toward the parking area. I put my hand on

Houston's forehead. "You look really pale. Are you sure you're okay?"

"I'm fine." He brushed a lock of my hair from my cheek. "You look pretty pale yourself. Are you okay?"

"I'm fine. A little headachy, but fine."

In reality, my head felt like a heavy metal band was playing inside my brain, but I didn't need to worry Houston with something he couldn't do a thing about.

When Ed returned with the map, we located the coordinates Landon had given us. "Do you know where this is?" I asked. It really did look like there was a whole lot of nothing.

"Yeah. It's north of here. Not much up that way. There is an old airstrip."

My brows shot up. "Airstrip. That has to be it."

Ed rolled up the map.

"Houston and I will take Dru's truck," I said. "We'll follow you and Mucker."

"The road is pretty rough," Ed warned.

"I'm sure we'll be fine," I assured him even though the thought of a drive along a bumpy road when my head already felt like my brain would literally spill out wasn't something I was looking forward to.

Houston offered to drive, but I reminded him that people with a concussion shouldn't operate heavy machinery, so he conceded and agreed that I should drive. Both our guns had been taken, but luckily, Ed had extras, so he provided each of us with a hunting rifle before we left the clinic. The road north hadn't been plowed, nor were there any road markers. If not for the fact that we were following Ed, I would never have been able to find the road.

The trip to the location where Landon had found Dru's cell phone wasn't a long one, but with the condition of the road, we had to take it slow, which was doubly frustrating since I kept picturing Dru fighting for his life alone in the dark, unaware that people were looking for him. There was one positive sign; however, as we arrived at the road we were looking for, there were fresh tracks in the snow, which indicated to me at least that we were on the right track.

As we neared the coordinates Landon had provided, we saw Dru's SUV in a ditch. A quick survey of the interior of the vehicle confirmed that Dru had indeed met with foul play. He'd been shot, and there was blood everywhere, but so far, he still had a pulse. Calling for an ambulance would take longer than if one of us simply drove him back to the clinic, so it was decided that Ed would take him back in his truck, and Houston and I would continue to the airstrip, which was located a few more miles down the road.

"You folks be careful," Ed called out as he pulled away from the side of the road after securing Dru inside his vehicle.

"We will," I said. "I hope Dru is going to be okay. I'll call you later."

Houston let out a little groan as we hit a bump. I'm not sure why that struck me as funny, but suddenly, I burst out laughing.

"Something funny?" Houston asked.

"No. Not at all. In fact, everything is really messed up. I'm not sure why I'm laughing, but it just struck me that as the go-to team out to capture the bad guy and save the day, we're pretty pathetic."

He smiled. "I guess we are. My head feels like a train is running around inside it, and while you keep saying you're fine, I can see that you aren't."

Fine wasn't even close to describing my current state of health, but we'd come this far, and one way or the other, I was seeing this through to the end.

When we arrived at the airstrip, a plane was sitting in what looked to be no more than an empty field. I pulled the truck off the road, Houston and I grabbed the hunting rifles Ed had loaned to us, and we went to investigate. The plane was empty, and to be honest, we weren't even a hundred percent certain that this plane was the means by which Carl planned to flee.

"Maybe we should wait for Carl to show up and grab him," I said.

Houston twisted his lips to the side. "Cause that worked so well the last time."

I smiled. "This time, we'll stay put and keep our eyes on the prize."

Houston hesitated.

"Do you have a better idea?" I asked.

"Actually, I don't. Let's hide the truck behind that grove of trees off to the side of the road. Hopefully, Carl will show up sooner rather than later. I'm not sure about you, but I'm ready for this to be over."

"Right there with you."

As it turned out, we had less than thirty minutes to wait. Carl pulled up in a truck just as another plane landed on the airstrip. Houston and I hadn't been planning to have two bad guys to capture, but it was what it was, so we slipped out of the truck and slowly made our way toward the plane closest to us. It was dark, and no one seemed to be looking for intruders, so we safely made it across the open field, where we hunkered down behind the wheel-well of the plane that we'd initially found empty. I really wasn't sure what to do at this point, and it seemed as if Houston wasn't either. I also wasn't sure how many people had arrived in the plane that had just landed. It did seem as if the plane we'd found when we arrived was the plane Carl had used to bring the girls from Huntsville to Barron. Emily had let me know that Carl could fly, so it made sense that he piloted the plane himself to the airstrip and then stashed the girls in town while he waited for his contact.

I felt an urge to do something but decided to follow Houston's lead and just wait. We each had a hunting rifle, but we knew Carl had more than one gun, and the addition of the second plane made things tricky. We watched as Carl approached the plane that had just landed. We watched as a man got out and approached Carl. I assumed the man in the second plane was the man who planned to buy the girls. I couldn't hear what was being said, but it was apparent that the conversation had grown heated. Carl pulled his gun, but before he could get off a round, the man who'd arrived in the second plane shot him. I got up, prepared to confront the man, but Houston grabbed my arm. I hated to do nothing other than watch as the man who shot Carl flew away, but Houston had seen two more men come to the door of the plane just as the man who shot Carl turned to re-board.

Once the plane was gone, we jogged over to check on Carl, who, we confirmed, was good and dead.

"Wow," I said as I stood standing in the dark snowy night, unsure of what to do at this point. "That did not go how I thought it would."

"No, it didn't," Houston said.

"I hate that they got away."

Houston put his arm around my shoulder. "I know. I do too, but there were three of them, all with guns. They had the advantage, and I think our poor bodies have already been through enough to risk getting shot."

"At least we saved the girls," I said, laying my head on his shoulder.

"Yes, we did. And in the end, that's what really matters."

I looked down at our kidnapper. "What do we do with him?"

Houston picked him up and tossed him over his shoulder. "We'll take him back to town, turn him over to Ed, and let local law enforcement figure it out from there."

"Do you think there's an empty hotel room anywhere in that little town?" I asked as I walked beside Houston back to Dru's truck.

"Lord, I hope so. I really don't think I can stay awake much longer."

"A shower would be nice."

"A shower would be wonderful," Houston agreed.

Chapter 16

It had been a week since Houston and I had returned to Rescue. All the girls had been returned to their homes, and Jeremy was still staying with Jake and Jordan. Houston had done some digging and had been able to find out that Jeremy's father had actually sold Jeremy to Carl, which is why he never initiated a missing persons report. If not for the neighbor, we might never have had the information we did that allowed us to identify the boy. Jake hadn't been in the market for a roommate or a part-time employee, but he confided in me that there was no way he was going to let the boy go back to his father. The apartment over the bar where I'd lived before I bought my cabin was empty, so Jake cleaned it up, and Jeremy settled in there.

Despite the fact that Jeremy had only been with Jake for a little over a week, the two had already worked out a series of hand signals that allowed them to communicate just fine. If there was one good thing that had come from this whole fiasco, it was that Jeremy had finally been rescued after four years of servitude to a monster.

"So it sounds like it all worked out," Harley said after I told him my story. I'd been trying to get in touch with him for a week, but his film crew had temporarily moved to an island off the coast of California, and apparently, no one had cell service. There were satellite radios that could be used in an emergency, but Harley hadn't felt the need to check-in, so he hadn't asked to use one.

"Everything did work out okay," I said. "Dru is going to be fine. In fact, I spoke to him this morning, and he's already out of the hospital. The men in the second plane did get away, which I hate, and we don't even know who they were, so we have no way to try to track them down, which I doubly hate, but we did save the girls and Jeremy, so I suppose this case can be recorded in the win column."

"I would say this case was definitely a win. How have you been feeling since you've been back?"

"Better. The headaches are mostly gone. I still get a twinge every now and then, but I feel like the pain is less with each day that goes by. Houston is fine as well, so I guess at this point, I can report that all is well."

"I can't believe I missed everything."

"I can't believe you allowed yourself to be taken to an island with no cell service and internet. It must have made you nuts."

"Actually, it wasn't bad," Harley answered. "When we first arrived and were told that satellite radios would be the only means of communication, everyone went berserk. I thought Loretta was literally going to burst a blood vessel, but after everyone got used to the idea, it wasn't so bad. I guess I'm used to the spotty cell and internet service at home, so I adapted the quickest. It was actually nice to unplug a bit, but I did miss talking to you every day."

"I missed you too, but to be honest, with everything that was going, on I'm not sure we would have been able to have these two-hour gab sessions anyway." I smiled as I looked out the window at the snow that had started to fall. "Do you think it's strange that we talk so long when you are on a shoot? We don't talk for two hours every day when you're here in town."

"I see you almost every day when I'm in town."

"That's true, I guess."

"How are the kittens? Have you had a chance to check in with Serena?"

"I have, and the kittens are great. Really, really cute. I'm sorry they will have all been rehomed by the time you get home. You're going to miss them completely, but there's always another litter around the corner."

"Especially with spring just around the corner."

Harley and I continued to chat for another hour. By the time we hung up, he was all caught up, and I was ready to settle in for the night with my menagerie of animals. I hadn't spoken to Houston for a couple of days and was considering calling him before I became too settled when there was a knock on the door.

"I hope you haven't eaten." Houston held up a pizza box and a bottle of wine.

"I haven't." I stepped aside. "And that pizza smells amazing." I closed the door behind him. "Did we discuss getting together tonight?"

"No. I got off work and was hungry. I decided to pick up pizza and realized that you might not have eaten and might want some, so I headed in this direction."

"How very spontaneous of you." I grabbed two plates from the cupboard.

"Being spontaneous isn't my strong suit, but I have decided to try out some new things now that we're into the new year."

I took a sip of my wine. "Oh. Like what?"

He looked me directly in the eye. "I've lived here for a few years now, and in all that time, I've never seen you date anyone. Do you date?"

I frowned.

"I mean, you don't have a personal policy against dating, do you?"

"No, I don't have a policy against dating. Why do you ask?" I looked at the wine. "Is this a date?"

"No. This is just pizza. I haven't dated since my divorce, but it occurred to me that it might be time. If, at some point in the future, I decided it might be time to start dating again, would you be open to going on a date with me?"

I smiled. "I don't know. When you're ready, why don't you ask me, and I guess we'll see how it all works out."